CRUISE WITH AN ADORABLE FAT GIRL

Bernice Bloom

Published internationally by Gold Medals Media Ltd:

CONTENTS

3rd May 2018

Dear Ms Brown,

Thank you for arranging to come on the 20 day Mediterranean cruise with Angel Cruises. We look forward to welcoming you and Ms Dawn Walters on board and hope you enjoy the holiday of a lifetime with us.

The ship will be leaving Southampton at 5pm (BST) and boarding will start at 2pm. All the information about your cruise, and the ship, is enclosed, along with details about our on-shore excursions and events. If you have any questions, please do not hesitate to contact us.

We look forward to seeing you on Monday 7th June.

Kind regards,

Captain Homarus & the crew of The Angel of the Seas

7th May 2018

Dear Ms Brown,

Thank you very much for your reply to my letter.

I can confirm that there is an 'eat-as-much-as-you-possibly-can' buffet on board, the bar is open all day and there is a mini bar in every cabin. We will make sure that it is stocked with plenty of gin and snacks, as you request.

We look forward to meeting you.

Kind regards,

Captain Homarus & the crew of Angel of the Seas

10th May 2018

Dear Ms Brown,

Thank you very much for your letter.

We will certainly make sure that there's a variety of snacks in the room, and not just 'those daft peanuts in a tin'. We also take on board your point about leaving a measly chocolate on your pillow. If we wish to leave you chocolates we will, as you suggest, leave you a whole box next to your bed and not in it.

We look forward to meeting you.

Kind regards,

Captain Homarus & the crew of Angel of the Seas

ITINERARY: 20 DAY MEDITERRANEAN CRUISE

Departure: Southampton
First stop: Lisbon
Second stop: Gibraltar
Third stop: Tunisia
Fourth stop: Sardinia
Fifth stop: Malta
Sixth stop: Sicily
Seventh stop: Naples
Eighth stop: La Spezia
Ninth stop: Toulon
Tenth stop: Barcelona
Eleventh stop: Valencia
Twelfth stop: Southampton

CHAPTER ONE: PREPARING TO LEAVE

The first thing I did was tell mum: "You won't believe this," I said, breathless with excitement, "I'm going on a cruise."

There was an overly long pause while she put down the steaming iron and worked out how to reply.

"A cruise? What - like a big boat?" she offered.

"Yep," I said. "A very big boat. It's got restaurants, a pub, a tennis court and swimming pools on it."

"OK," she said, looking at the basket full of crumpled clothes, then at me.

"Will you be gone all day?"

"It's a 20 day cruise, mum. I'll be gone for most of the month. Dawn invited me. Remember Dawn? The girl I was at school with who's now a successful blogger."

"Yes - of course I remember Dawn. You went on safari with her and it all went pear-shaped."

"Yep - that's the one."

"You wrote a blog called Two Fat Ladies and ended up stuck up a tree in your knickers."

"Yep - that's the one."

"And my bridge club was round here when I opened the blog up to show them and they were treated to the unusual sight of your bottom as you clambered out of a tree while half drunk. Marjorie's never forgotten it."

"Yes, yes. No need to go back over all that, mum. Well Dawn's invited me on a cruise ship now and there are no trees on cruise ships, nor are there baboons, so I'm confident that there won't be a repeat of the knicker-wearing nonsense. It's going to be free because I'm her guest for the trip and she'll be blogging about it. Dawn gets to take someone with her every time. I've had letters from the captain confirming it. It's definitely happening. There's a massive 'eat all you can' buffet and everything."

"It's called 'eat all you want', not 'eat all you can' - you make it sound like some sort of competition. And you'll need to watch yourself with those buffets. You don't want to put on any more weight. You'll come back 16 stone if you're not careful."

I didn't want to point out that I was 19 stone, so to come back 16 stone would be a very marvellous thing indeed, probably involving some sort of gastric bypass surgery along the way.

"Do you want to know what countries I'm going to?"

"Go on then," she said, and I listed the glamorous locations where the luxury cruise ship would stop. I mentioned Sicily and Barcelona and she ironed dad's pants while I told about Gibraltar and the tantalising thought of Tunisia and Lisbon.

"Pass me those shirts," she said.

"Mum, are you listening to any of this?"

"Yes, dear. Pass the starch as well."

She seemed more concerned with getting creases out of y-fronts and starching shirts than hearing about the glamour of life on the ocean wave, so I gave up and went to put the kettle on.

It was two days later when she called me in a state of near hysteria.

"I'm calling from Walker & Sons - the travel agents on Barnes Road."

"Right," I said. "Everything OK?"

"Yes, I'm here with your Aunty Susan. We've been looking at the brochures for cruises. Goodness me, Mary Brown. They are lovely."

"I know. They are, aren't they?"

I was in Marks and Spencer at the time, looking at bright red, plunging bikinis, and trying to summon up the nerve to go and try one on.

"They have theatres and ballrooms and EVERYTHING," mum was saying.

"Yep," I said, holding the tiny bikini up against my large frame and trying to ignore the distasteful glances from the assistants.

"Well, you make sure you have a lovely time, won't you. I've never seen anything like this. A pub on a ship! Is that even legal?"

"I think so" I said, putting the bikini back on the rack and picking up a sober, structured swimming costume that might actually fit me. "I'll let you know all about it when I get back."

"OK, dear," said mum. "Do be careful though, won't you. You know what you're like. You'll have too many cocktails, trip over your flip flops and fall overboard or something."

"I promise I won't," I said. "I won't wear flip flops if there's alcohol around."

"Good girl," said mum. "You have a good time."

"I will," I said, putting down the swimming costume and reaching for an outsized kaftan.

"Love you lots, mum."

So, all goodbyes had been said, three weeks had been booked off work, and I'd packed a colossal amount of clothing into a massive suitcase. Ted, my lovely, long-suffering boyfriend had agreed to take me down to Southampton Docks, so we went bouncing into the car park in his dilapidated old Mini Micra. The car's not really stable enough for two adults, let alone two obese ones. I'd taken to wearing a sports bra and clutching my breasts on long journeys because the damn thing bounced so much.

Ted drove round the car park, directed by a series of men in fluorescent vests, until he was shown a parking place facing the harbour. "Look at that!" he gasped, pointing to the ship in front of us. "Wow it looks impressive."

My goodness it did too. It looked amazing. The sun beat down on the sparkling water and there in the middle of it all was this incredible ship: *Angel of the Seas*...my home for the next three weeks. It was massive. MASSIVE. It demanded a full head turn to follow it from end to end. I don't know what I was expecting, but this was awesome.

I could hardly believe what was happening...it was a beautiful warm, early summer's day and I was going off on a Mediterranean cruise, and it was all free. Dawn had to be the best friend in the world. I mean – she was nuts, and had been slightly uncomfortable company at times when we were on safari, but – a free cruise! I could put up with a bit of Dawn madness for that.

I clambered out of the car and felt a shot of excitement rush through me. This was just thrilling. I started to waddle off towards the ship at full speed until Ted stopped me.

"Haven't you forgotten something?" he said.

"Have I? My passport? Sun cream? Sun dresses?"

"No, a kiss. Where's my kiss goodbye?"

"Oh yes – sorry!" I said, rushing back and throwing myself into his arms, hugging him closely. "I'm going to miss you."

"Yes – I'm sure you will," said Ted, sarcastically. "I'm sure you'd much rather be in the pub with me than exploring the delights of Tunisia and Lisbon."

"I'm not sure about that," I said. "But I really wish you were coming with me."

"Me too," he said, stroking my hair tenderly. "I don't feel like we've spent any time together recently, what with you off on safari and me working so hard. Promise me we can see each other loads when you get back."

"I promise," I said. "And I'll text you and call you to let you know how it's all going."

"Make sure you do," said Ted. "I want to know everything."

"You will. I love you."

"I love you, too," said Ted, finally letting go of me and wishing me bon voyage.

Bloody hell...it was all real – I was actually going on a cruise!

CHAPTER TWO: HANDSOME CAPTAIN & A MASSIVE BUFFET

B_{y the} time I stepped onto the ship I was already head over heels in love with cruising. It's all incredibly easy. You check in quickly and wander onboard, unencumbered by any of your bags which are delivered directly to your cabin. Easy. None of the faff that's usually associated with international travel. No angry customs officials or mind-bendingly long queues. There weren't endless shops at the departure point either, which was a blessing. I can't be trusted around those airport shops. I have more orange lipstick, glittery highlighter and green eyeliner from those things than I could use in a lifetime. The stuff you buy when you're all excited and waiting to go on holiday is the sort of stuff you would never normally go anywhere near. I have makeup that would look perfect were I ever invited to perform in the Mardi Gras, or join Abba circa 1978, but is entirely unsuitable for my life as a checkout girl at a DIY and garden centre in Cobham.

Anyway - all I'm saying is that it was a small mercy that there were no shops to drive me wild and it was lovely that it was so easy to board.

I stepped onto the ship to the sounds of a string quartet playing soothingly in the background. The captain was there to greet us, a strikingly handsome man with all the suave sophistication you'd expect of a man in his position.

"Good morning, Madam. Welcome to the Angel of the Seas. My name's Will Homarus," he said. "I'm your captain for this cruise."

"Good morning," I said back, curtseying slightly which was highly embarrassing. Something about the uniform and the majesty of the ship made me behave as if I was meeting royalty.

Will was reassuringly good-looking. Big and manly, kind of swarthy, like he might be Greek or something. He certainly looked like he could save us all if things went pear-shaped.

"The boat's not going to sink is it? " I said, because I do have a habit of saying ridiculous things to handsome men.

"No, you're quite safe," he said, smiling. I knew instantly that I would have to keep right away from this guy when I'd had a few glasses of wine or I'd be wrapping my legs round his neck and asking him to marry me.

"I'm Claire Oliver," said an attractive woman standing next to him. She was tall and painfully thin. I didn't really want to talk to her. I was much happier talking to the Greek God with the hairy chest but he'd turned away and was greeting the next passengers: a rather dour-looking woman in a brown dress and an ancient man in a wheelchair.

"I'm the staff captain," she said. "Kind of like the deputy captain. We'll both be around the ship, so do talk to us if there's anything you need or if there are any problems."

"Yes, I will," I said, trying to catch the captain's eye, but he was crouched down, talking to the guy in the wheelchair, so I gave up and told Claire that 'yes, of course, I'll come and find one of you if I needed anything.' I was very sure which one of them I'd be going to find and it wasn't Claire.

A lovely young man called David showed me to my cabin, opening the door and leading me into a gorgeous room with two beds, a bathroom, and - joy of joys - a sea view. I rushed to the patio doors and flung them open.

"It's the sea," I said.

"It is," said David. "There's sea all around. Is it OK if I go now?"

"Of course," I said, slightly embarrassed that I sounded as if I didn't I understand how boats worked.

I texted Dawn as soon as he closed the door behind him: "OMG. I've just walked into the cabin...it's bloody lovely...see you soon. M x"

Then I did what every self-respecting woman does in a situation like this: I opened the mini bar, pulled out a toblerone and a mini bottle of gin and tonic and threw myself onto the bed to work out how the TV operated.

My God, the bed was soft...it was like lying in cotton wool. I snuggled down into it and watched the video on the screen about life aboard the ship.

There was a beautician that looked amazing...like a proper New York spa. It even did Botox. I rolled over and peered into the mirror by the bed, holding my eyebrows up to see what I'd look like. Was that better? Or did I just look like a fat Chinese woman? It was hard to tell. Probably best not to take the risk though. They did manicures and facials as well which I definitely wanted to try.

Next they showed the gym and fitness suite and the classes that took place every day. If I went to the gym every morning and did regular beauty treatments, I could go home from this cruise looking amazing, especially if I got some sun on my skin as well. That would be great.

Then the video moved to the buffets that would be available for breakfast and lunch. My God! In an instant I knew that far from returning home having lost a few pounds, there was every chance that I would return home 10 stone heavier. The meat. All the Chinese food. Ooooo...I just love Chinese food. And the puddings! Have you seen these buffets? Miles of tables groaning under the weight of all the food. On the video they showed a slim, young lady going to the buffet and helping herself to a light salad and a sliver of smoked salmon.

No woman can do that.

It's not possible to go to an eat-all-you-can buffet and return with a sensible plate of food. Whenever I'm confronted by them I panic and end up with a plate of roast potatoes, chips, pasta, chicken in black bean sauce, cheese, prawn toast, fried egg and sprouts, or something...food that has no right to be sharing crockery.

The sight of all the food had made me a little peckish, so I finished my drink, slipped my shoes on and wandered out of the cabin. When I got outside, my case was sitting there with a little note on it, wishing me an excellent holiday. This was perfect...so easy and smooth. Three weeks of this and I'd return home totally relaxed and stress-free. Assuming, of course, that the rest of the holiday went as smoothly as this first day had.

I walked up to the buffet and saw Captain Homarus. He was putting a delicate collection of olives, little silver skin onions and some fancy cheese onto his plate. He must have been watching the girl on the video. I smiled at him and started placing items onto my plate in a similar fashion. As soon as he was out of sight, I'd start digging into the lasagne and make a serious dent in the chips.

"Do come and join me," he said, indicating the table by the window in the corner.

"That would be lovely," I said, thinking of the fried chicken and potato wedges I'd have to forsake. "I'll just get a drizzle of olive oil and I'll be right with you."

I walked the length of the buffet, picking at delicacies as I went; a spring roll went into my mouth, then a handful of chips. I grabbed a burger to eat while walking round. I bit into luscious beef, while dropping two slivers of sun-dried tomato onto my plate. I don't know who I thought I was kidding, really. No sane person could I believe that I ate in the way my plate indicated. I wouldn't be morbidly obese if my diet consisted of delicately flavoured olives and bits of tomato, would I?

Still, one had to keep up appearances. I took a glug of water to wash down the last of the burger, wiped my face, and headed to the corner table. But when I looked, he wasn't there. There were three people sitting there, chatting away.

Where was he? I have a terrible sense of direction, and I'd wandered up and down the buffet that ran the length of the boat. Now I didn't know where to go. Which corner was he in? There were so many nooks and crannies. I walked up and down. I asked the chefs whether they'd seen him but they shook their heads, I asked a couple of fellow passengers but - no - no one had seen him. I was completely lost. In the end I had to get them to put a message over the tannoy for him to come and find me. By the time he reached me, I'd been gone for 20 minutes. He'd eaten his cocktail onions and had been sitting there patiently, wondering where on earth I'd got to.

"Sorry," I said, exasperated. "I got lost."

"No problem at all," he said patiently. "Come and join me."

He was on the other side of the boat entirely.

I stayed with Handsome Homarus until I'd finished my food, then he excused himself and went back to work. The minute he was out of sight I loaded my plate with every different Chinese food on the buffet, and then I ate the whole plateful quicker than anyone has ever eaten a plateful of food in their life before and practically rolled back to my cabin, feeling like I might explode. I lay on the bed, poured myself another gin and tonic, wished I hadn't eaten so much and downed the drink to make myself feel better. Then I read my messages. There was one from Ted, wishing me bon voyage, and one from Dawn.

"Hi darling," it said. "Can you call me urgently?"

I picked up my phone and glanced at the time. It was 4pm. We were setting sail soon. Where the hell was she? I dialled her number and there was a terrible noise when she answered it.

"Dawn, it's me," I said. "Dawn, can you hear me?"

The noise stopped. "Yes, sorry - I was just getting a blow dry. How are you?"

"I'm fine but shouldn't you be - like - on the ship instead of in the hairdressers?"

"Oh darling, I'm so sorry - that's why I was ringing - I can't make it. Something's come up. Could you write the blog for me?"

"Whaaat?"

"It'll be fine," she said.

"Errr...no it won't, because I'm not a writer. I've never written anything longer than a Christmas card before."

"You can do it," she said. "Just send me text updates with what's going on, and I'll load them onto the blog. No one will be any the wiser."

"OK," I said, struggling to keep the concern out of my voice. "So I literally just send you texts with what's going on, and that's all I need to do."

"Yep," she said. "Simple eh?"

"Yes, that does sound quite straightforward," I agreed.

"Oh, one other thing," she added. "Don't tell anyone that I'm not there. Just pretend I'm in the cabin if anyone asks. OK?"

"What? I can't spend 20 days telling everyone that you're in the cabin."

"Tell them I've just left or I'm in the hairdressers or having a lie down, or getting my nails done. Use your imagination. It'll be fine. Have fun. Just don't tell anyone that I'm not on the boat though please or I won't get any more free trips."

Christ.

CHAPTER THREE: MEETING THE GUESTS

As the ship prepared to move out of the harbour, we were all encouraged to go onto the deck for a setting sail party. This event involved glasses of fizz, excitement, singing and flag waving - all things of which I approve entirely, so I was there like a shot. It was also a chance to get to know the other shipmates, so I wandered around, introducing myself and sending texts to Dawn, updating her on what was going on and who I was meeting, so she could write about it in the blog.

"Pictures!" she texted back. "Send pictures."

"No one mentioned that," I replied.

"We definitely need pictures, and videos are VITAL. The blog will fall flat and no one will read it and neither of us will get any free holidays ever again if you don't send me videos."

Great. Now I had to be Steven Spielberg as well as JK Rowling. So much for a free holiday.

I held my phone up and took a video of all the guests singing and waving their flags, and then I moved it round slightly to capture the sight of Captain Homarus bending over to tie up his shoes. I confess I lingered on that shot slightly longer than was necessary, but panned back out to take in the whole boat before he saw. "Video attached," I wrote, texting it to Dawn.

"Hot, hot, hot!" she replied.

"Thank you."

"Not you. The dude in the tight, white trousers."

"He's called the captain."

"Wish I was there," she typed.

"Glad you're not. I have him all to myself," I typed back, texting it to her with a still from the video of his manly bottom.

The downside of chatting to people was being forced to explain to them about Dawn: "No, I'm not on my own, I'm with my friend but she's in the cabin, feeling unwell."

"Oh dear," they all said, before asking exactly what was wrong with her.

"Just illness, you know," I replied vaguely, looking at them with great seriousness, so they didn't probe further. What I lacked in medical nous, I made up for with steely gazing.

I sent Dawn another video of the ship leaving Southampton harbour, and of all the happy cruisers cheering, waving and singing Rule Britannia and land of Hope and Glory, and then I went back to the cabin to get dressed for the evening.

Cruise ships have very strict sartorial guidelines, as Dawn had been at pains to point out to me. Even on the 'dress down' nights, women tend to wear cocktail dresses. On the black tie evenings, it's full-on long dresses, sparkly handbags, mink stoles and long gloves. I have all of these things...incase you were wondering. I LOVE getting dressed up. My stoles aren't real mink, and my sparkly shoes and matching handbag don't have a diamond on them, but I look the part all the same.

For that first evening I went for a long red dress that was designed for a woman with a far smaller bust than I have. I rammed my assets into it and looked in the mirror. "Oh no," I thought. "All you can see is blonde hair, red dress and enormous breasts."

Then I stopped for a minute and thought, 'No - that's a good thing. I will be very popular tonight if all you can see is blonde hair, red dress and enormous breasts.'

The positive thinking (coupled with the gin) gave me a real confidence boost, and I walked down to the gorgeous, art deco-style dining room swaying with delight and swinging my hair back. I stopped for a gin and tonic at the bar first, and then sauntered over to the table at which I'd been told I was dining.

It turned out it was the captain's table which meant I'd be having lunch and dinner with Handsome Captain Homarus. Not a bad start to the holiday.

I glanced at the floor-to-ceiling mirrors by the table. I seemed to have 'dropped' a little in the walk over. I shoved my hand down the front and hitched up my boobs so they sat better in the dress, giving me a more attractive cleavage. I did this just as Claire, the deputy captain, came over to say hello. The wide-eyed look and little gasp she gave made me realise that I'd released a little too much flesh to the world. I looked down. Yep - It looked like two small bald men were trying to peek out of the top of my dress. I smiled at Claire and pushed them down again...kneading them as if I were preparing dough for the oven.

"This is your seat here," she said, politely ignoring the rigorous adjustments I was making, and pointing to a chair on the other side of the table from her.

I stood next to my seat as other guests drifted over to join us. There was a couple called Edith and Malcolm who looked like they were in their early 60s. They were the sort of people who were very helpful in life. Do you know the type I mean? You find them on every committee in every borough in the country...real salt of the earth types. Probably members of the tennis club and the church organising committee - she does the flowers and organises the summer fete, and he plays golf on Fridays. Nice people. Like my Aunty Susan. Nice, but not necessarily the sort of people you'd choose to join for dinner.

Next to me was the man who'd followed me onto the boat earlier - very, very old and frail and in a wheelchair. He smiled weakly and I bent down to introduce myself. He nodded like he couldn't hear me properly and said his name was Tank. An odd name, but quite nice for a little old man to be called something so powerful and evocative - I liked it.

Next to him sat the dour, plain-looking woman who'd pushed him onto the boat earlier. She had mousy hair which fell limply by her face, large, square glasses and was dressed in what looked like a uniform from the Brownies, or a nurse's outfit from years ago - like the sort of thing they wore on Call The Midwife. Her shoulders were massive - like an American Footballer's. Perhaps it was all that wheelchair pushing that did it?

"I'm Mary," I said, and she nodded without offering her name.

"How long have you known Tank?" I asked her.

"Tank?" she said.

"Yes, your friend," I indicated the man in the wheelchair.

"His name's Frank," she said.

"Oh, sorry. I misheard." She looked at me as if I'd just confessed to killing babies and chopping up kittens.

Meanwhile Frank just smiled, and nodded, not looking at me or anyone else. His red-rimmed eyes watered as he looked off into the distance. He was warm and friendly but not quite with it, somehow. Very different from the others at the table, most of whom seemed to have been invited because they were regular cruise goers, and knew the captain. On the other side of the table they were raucous and lively and sharing jokes. This side? Not so much. I looked at Frank while Frank looked down at his shaking hands.

"What made you come on a cruise, then?" I asked.

He smiled at me again, and the lady with the large shoulders and bad dress leaned over and fiddled with what I imagined to be his hearing aid.

"I can hear now," he said with a broad smile. "What were you saying, dear?"

"I just asked why you were on the cruise."

"Oh. You don't want to know," he said. "It's a very long story."

"Of course I want to know," I said, but he just smiled at me and the lady next to him began feeding him. We fell silent as he chewed his food and I began to eat mine. To be honest, I didn't much want to know. I was only being polite.

Once Frank had finished eating, the woman wiped his face gently. "Tell her your story, Frank," she said. "Tell her why we're on the cruise."

"I'm here because I'm off to Tunisia say a proper goodbye to two old friends...and then to Sicily to apologise to the family of the love of my life."

"Oh. Why do you have to say goodbye to your friends?" I asked.

"My friends died in the war. I was fighting beside them when they were gunned down on a rainy night. One guy died where he fell, the other died in a military hospital soon afterwards. I want to go back to where we lost them on that bleak hill on that bleak night and say goodbye properly, forever, before I die."

"Oh my God, that's so moving," I said, feeling tears in the backs of my eyes. "Really moving and so sad."

"It was war," he said, with a distant smile. "Sad things happened."

"And did you say something about the family of the woman you loved?"

"Yes, I need to make amends. I took her away from them in the dead of night. I need to go back and apologise, and to hand them the letters from 70 odd years ago that were never sent. It's the right thing to do...I need to give them the letters"

"Come on Frank," said the woman in the brown dress. "It's time for you to go to bed now."

"No, not yet," I said, now genuinely intrigued. "Can't he tell me the story first? Tell me about the letters...I don't understand."

"In time, my dear," said Frank with a lovely, big smile. "I'll tell you everything. It's a long cruise. No need to rush things."

"Oh but - I have no patience at all. Please tell me now."

"He will tell you everything, but not now," said the woman in the horrible dress, pushing the wheelchair away.

"OK," I said, reluctantly, turning my attention to the glass of wine in front of me, and the captivating smile of Captain H, but I couldn't stop thinking about Frank. What letters? What apology? It was so intriguing. And imagine losing your best friends like that. It was beyond comprehension.

CHAPTER FOUR: EN ROUTE TO LISBON

Oh God. Oh God. It was so bright. Where was I? What happened? My head felt like it was spontaneously combusting from within. My tongue was so dry it was as if I'd spent the previous evening licking the carpets. I couldn't have done that...could I? It wasn't beyond the realm of possibilities; I'd had worse nights.

The light in my cabin was on full blast, and the sun was streaming through the window. It was bright enough to perform brain surgery. I crawled across the bed and lashed out at the lamp and the main light switch. I was still too drunk to execute any subtle manoeuvres but eventually, after much swatting, the lights went out and I crashed out across the bed and went to sleep. When I woke up it was 10.30am.

There was just half an hour left before the sumptuous breakfast buffet became the sumptuous lunchtime buffet. I needed to move.

Slowly I stumbled out of bed and dressed myself rather like a toddler picking the first top I saw in the wardrobe (green) and the nearest trousers (pink) with complete disregard for how they would look together.

I wandered cautiously along the corridor and took the lift up to the main deck. Every step made my head hurt more. I needed coffee...and food, but then I always needed food. I stepped out of the lift and saw a man, standing with his back to me, but with his reflection clearly visible in the glass in front of him.

Oh my f-ing God, it was Simon Collins. Simon Collins!

It was like being shot back in time.

I reversed into the lift and pressed the button to the lower floor, pushing it a thousand times, urging the doors to close, but they were too slow - Simon looked up, saw me in the mirror in front of him; his eyes widened, his eyebrows raised and he spun round just as the door was closing.

"Mary?" he said, with incredulity sweeping through his voice. "Mary? Really, is that you? Mary Brown. In the pink trousers?"

If I was surprised to see Simon, then he was a million more times surprised to see me...for the simple fact that four years ago I'd told him that I had six months to live. I know, I know, it's appalling behaviour but I'm rubbish at finishing relationships and I just came out with it.

I'd told Simon that I no longer wanted to see him, adding; "it's not you, it's me." And he'd said 'no, it's not Mary - that's a stupid thing to say - it's me. It must be me. If there wasn't something wrong with me, you'd want to carry on going out with me."

Dear readers, I panicked at this stage and I said 'yes - it *is* me...I've got leprosy.'

"Leprosy," he'd said, jumping back, his little face awash with concern. "Blimey, that sounds really serious."

My lies kicked off more lies and before I knew where I was, I was explaining that I was going off to Fiji in search of a witch doctor. I know - it was bizarre. I don't know what made me say it. I was in a panic because I hate upsetting people. I suppose I thought I could get away with it because Simon lived in Birmingham where he was working at the university, so there was no chance of us bumping into one another. He called a few of times to check I was OK but I'd begged him to get on with his own life and leave me to my fate.

Now, here he was, on the bloody ship with me, and there was no way of me escaping.

I stepped out of the lift on the cabin floor, went back to my room and texted Charlie, my lovely friend who'd been in on the whole witch doctor thing (if memory serves me right, she'd jumped around in the background making 'witch doctor noises' one time when he'd called and I'd pretended to be on a Fijian island).

"You are joking. That is hysterical," she said, rather unsupportively. "God, I wish I was there to see this. His face must have been a picture!"

"Yep. He did look very shocked," I said. "How do I get out of this?"

"Tell him you got better. Insist that the witch doctor performed his magic and the illness disappeared."

"Yeah, I could," I said. "Or I could just avoid him."

"Yeah - well, of course, if you can avoid him - do that, but I don't fancy your chances on a 20 day cruise."

"Yeah," I said. "What I'll do is try to avoid him, and if I can't, I'll go for the witch doctor line."

"Perfect," said Charlie. "What could possibly go wrong?"

I couldn't risk going back up to breakfast, so I had to miss it and wait until lunchtime (exactly 20 minutes, so it didn't involve my internal organs collapsing due to lack of nutrition or anything but it felt quite a long time for a girl who likes her food), then I went back up on deck when I knew that breakfast was over. I used the lifts on the other side of the ship instead of risking exiting at exactly the point where I'd seen Simon earlier. I don't really know why I did that, it wasn't as if Simon would have stood in that position all day, but it just seemed safer, somehow, to avoid going where I knew he'd been. I strode out of the lift and over to the buffet, avoiding looking at everyone in the misguided belief that if I didn't see anyone, then no one could see me. It's a tactic used by every toddler who's ever played hide and seek.

Once at the buffet, I started loading chicken wings and nuggets onto my plate along with noodles and curry sauce. I figured I was allowed to go a little bit mad because I hadn't had any breakfast. Also, I'd been drinking the night before and every right-thinking person knows that a little indulgence is a must the day after massive drinking has happened. It's practically the only way to make yourself feel better again.

I wandered over to sit down when I caught sight of Frank and his nurse (I assumed she was his nurse, based on her dress sense and bossy attitude, but to be honest, she hadn't even given me her name, let alone her occupation).

"Hello, do you mind if I join you?" I said, giving them both a big smile.

"Of course not," said Frank, beaming. His craggy face came alive when he smiled.

"I was just hearing about you," he said.

"Were you?"

"Yes, the captain was telling that you were performing *YMCA* last night and doing high kicks to *New York, New York*. You were quite the party animal by the sound of it."

"Oh God, no."

"The captain said your Elvis impression was one of the best he'd ever seen."

"Oh hell. Tell me about your evening, Frank. Let's not dwell on mine anymore."

"Well it was a bit quieter than yours by the sound of it. No doing the can-can all the way round the boat for me."

"Right, good. Glad to hear it."

"I don't think she wants to be reminded about last night," said lady in brown dress. "We all drink too much from time to time, the last thing you need is for someone to remind you of all the details of it the next day."

"Fair enough," said Frank, with a nod of his head. "That's a good point."

I smiled appreciatively at her. "I'm so sorry, I don't even know your name," I said.

"It's Janette," she replied. "You can call me Jan."

"I will. Thanks," I said, then I asked: "Are you Frank's nurse?"

"No, I'm not," she said. "Not really, though I am a nurse, but I'm here as Frank's friend. He knew my grandfather very well and our families have become the best of friends."

There were more and more people coming along to the buffet, and I was sure I could see Simon in the group. Either that or I was being paranoid. Too many people were wearing navy blue t-shirts and shorts...it was going to be very hard to avoid him when I couldn't pick him out of a crowd.

I looked at Frank who was looking down at a piece of paper in his hands.

"What's that?"

"Irene," he said, lifting up the paper. It was a picture of a very beautiful woman with dark eyes and raven hair, set in old-fashioned curl around her shoulders. She had a huge smile. Like a movie star.

"She was the love of my life," he said.

"Is this the woman you mentioned last night? The one whose family you are going back to find and apologise to?"

"That's right," he said. "You have a good memory."

"You were going to tell me all about why you have to go back there, do you remember? You said you would tell me the whole story. "

"Of course I remember. Maybe I should tell you this evening, you must have things you want to do now. "

"No, please tell me now," I said. I didn't have anything else to do, and the thought of wandering around the boat had lost its appeal since I'd seen bloody Simon Collins. Frank squinted in my direction and began to talk. His voice was very soft; it was hard to hear everything that he was saying. I moved in closer to him.

"I'll have to take you right back to 1942 if I'm going to tell you the story properly," he said.

"Suits me," I said. "You can consider me firmly back in the 1940s."

"Well, I was 19 years old, living in a two up, two down in Portsmouth when I was called up to go and fight in the war."

"God, how awful. "

"No, not at all – I was thrilled. Especially when I was told I'd be going to North Africa with a group of other new recruits. I'd be joining the Eighth Army in Tunisia. The guys over there were known as the "desert rats". I'd heard about them on the wireless. They seemed incredibly glamorous.

"I'd never been abroad before, let alone to a different continent. And my family were so proud that I was going to fight for the country. No one else in the family had ever been to war. My father was injured so missed World War I, and it always hated himself for it. Until his dying day he felt less of a man because he hadn't been able to fight.

"None of it was his fault; he'd had had an industrial accident and had lost a foot. He also had limited use of his hand so of course he couldn't go to war. But he still felt terrible. I grew up with the idea that if you were a proper man you went to war and fought for your country. That's why it mattered so much to get the call up.

"I was super excited the day the papers came, and I was determined to make my parents proud. I didn't know, when I kissed them goodbye, and headed off to war that I would never see either of them again."

"Oh no."

Frank took a huge breath. "Yes, they were both killed in the bombings."

"Come on Frank," said Janette. "Time to go now..."

"Noooo.... Stay and tell me what happened. Please Frank, carry on. You've hardly started."

"Later," he said, as Janette started to push him away. "We have plenty of time, Mary Brown. Lots of time for storytelling."

CHAPTER FIVE: FIRST STOP - LISBON

There was something both frightening and exciting about coming in to dock for the first time. We'd all become so friendly on board that it seemed odd that we'd be mingling with other people who weren't part of our on board community. It was also exciting...we'd been cooped up for a few days - it was time to see the world. A frisson of excitement filtered through the group as we all queued up like children on a school trip, at the edge of the boat, looking out into the foreign port.

For me, it was a time of particularly mixed emotions, because while it was great fun to be coming in to port, I also reasoned that this was a time I was most likely to bump into Simon. That's why I had dressed incognito with a chiffon scarf over my head, entirely covering my hair, and large sunglasses.

"You look like that actress...what's her name?" said one of the guys. "You know - the blonde one?"

"Grace Kelly?" I said. That was certainly the look I'd been going for.

"No, no - Rebel Wilson," he said. "You look very like her."

"Thanks," I said. "I was hoping I was channelling Grace Kelly."

"Nope. Definitely Rebel Wilson."

As people stood, looking across the sparkling waters into the harbour, there was murmuring and chattering about the day ahead and what joys it might hold. People were making plans for what to do. I had no plans at all. I just wanted to see as much of the city as possible and post some interesting items on the blog so that Dawn would think I was a perfectly acceptable stand-in should she ever find herself unable to make a luxury holiday in the future.

It was odd to be facing the day in a strange city by myself but I'd read about the extraordinary number of ice cream parlours so I thought I'd probably be OK. One of the places was called Gelato Therapy which seemed to me to be the very best kind of therapy you could ever hope for.

We left the ship with strict instructions to be back by 5pm, having been told colourful stories of people who'd missed the ship in the past and ended up having to take flights to the next port. Their woeful antics seemed so frowned upon that we all swore we wouldn't be one of those people who broke the rules. We were advised to take passports and any essential medications with us though...just incase.

I left the ship and bid a fond farewell to handsome Captain Homarus, walking into the searing Portuguese sunshine with a huge smile on my face. It was surreal to be abroad when all I'd done was get on in Southampton, eaten a vast amount, drunk gallons and had a nice time, and now -ta-dah! – I was in a foreign place.

I walked off the ship with everyone else, clutching my map of Lisbon, and found my way to the narrow little streets leading up to the main road. It was very pretty: a cascade of houses rose up from the sea towards the castle at the top of the hill. From the beautiful blue waters of the harbour to the white houses with their caramel coloured roofs all stacked higgledy-piggledy, interspersed with lovely cafes, bars and rooftop restaurants, it was beautiful. Lisbon has the sort of buzz that you always get in cities, but with the added loveliness of being by the sea. How many capital cities are by the sea? Not many, I bet.

I walked up to a café sprawled across a rooftop and took a seat, looking down on our ship, sitting there majestically in the harbour. I watched the line of passengers snaking up the side of the hill. The café was so pretty that lots of the cruise passengers decided to come in and it was starting to feel a little like being back on the boat, and I kept thinking that Simon would walk in, so I turned quickly to the leaflet that the events co-ordinator had handed out, showing all the things that were happening in Lisbon, and decided it was time to make a plan. It seemed that the best way to see the place was either in a Tuk Tuk or by doing a circle of the city on a tram. Now I'm self-aware enough to know that if I got onto a Tuk-Tuk I'd break it, so I decided that the tram was the most sensible option.

I grabbed my bag and headed off for the tram stop. According to the literature there was one due in around 5 minutes.

Once it appeared, I clambered on board, took a seat by the window, and enjoyed the view as the tram snaked its way through the harbour streets, bouncing around on the rough, uneven roads and squeezing between large trucks that had no place to be out on these tiny, narrow lanes.

The tram took a turn up a hill dotted with houses in a range of chalky pastel colours.

"Well this is nice," I said, muttering the words out loud by mistake.

"It nice is yes," said a guy behind me. I swung round and found myself looking straight into deep brown eyes.

"Are you Portuguese?" I asked.

"Yes, I live Lisbon all life."

"All life?" I replied. "Oh, you Lisbon long time live."

I've no idea why I thought that mimicking his Pidgin English would somehow make me easier to understand, but I did.

"You are film star, yes?" he said.

I smiled at him warmly. "Thank you. No, I work in a gardening centre in Cobham."

"I have not seen this film," he said. "I will go."

"No, I work in a garden centre in Cobham. That's what I do."

"Yes, I always want to meet film star. I will watch all your film. What your name is?"

Now, come on, you have to accept that I tried to correct him. I tried to make him understand that I wasn't an international celebrity. I told him twice that I worked in a garden centre but he didn't seem to understand me. Hell, I was miles away from home...no one would know.

"My name is Rebel Wilson," I said.

"Well, I am Ernesto. It is nice to meet you Rachel."

"No - Rebel. My name is Rebel," I said, and then I went back to looking out at the views, examining a large black and white painting of a woman's face on the side of a building. Suddenly I felt my new friend by my side.

"I sorry, can I get picture with you, Rebel?"

"Of course," I said, adjusting my head scarf and posing next to him for a selfie.

"I will show you castle?" he said. "We get off here and I show you castle."

"No thank you," I said. "I'm going to stay on the tram."

"Yes, I show you castle," he said again. I seemed to have acquired a tour guide, but I wasn't really in the mood for old buildings, I wanted to hit the shops.

"I have to be back on my ship at 5pm," I told him. "So I have no time to see the castle."

"You have a ship! A film star ship."

"Um, well not really mine. It's the big ship in the harbour. Lots of people are on it...not just me."

"OK," he replied, as the tram reached the stop at the castle. "I go now." He stood up and began backing away from me, bowing slightly and holding his hands in the prayer position.

"I've just convinced a Portuguese guy that I'm a famous film star," I texted to Charlie.

"Was he blind?" she texted back. I need new friends.

After a few hours strolling through the streets, buying a new handbag and some candles and trying and failing to fit into a cream linen dress, I walked down the hill back towards the ship, loving the feeling of the sun on my skin as I walked. The sight of the gorgeous white houses with their caramel coloured roofs hit me again, and the beautiful blasts of pink flowers all set against the bright blue of the sea. I felt quite excited that I would be seeing Frank again. I hoped he'd been OK on the ship without us all. He'd said he was feeling too exhausted to get off, and would stay and make the most of having the whole place to himself to go swimming and relax.

As I walked to the ship I could see dozens of people lining up waiting by the passenger entrance. Why couldn't they get on, was something wrong?

Then there was a shout.

"There she is!"

I looked up and saw Ernesto, running towards me followed by cheering crowds of people.

"Rebel, Rebel, Rebel," they shouted excitedly. "We love you Rebel Wilson."

There were cheers and screams and begs for autographs and selfies. I looked up at the ship and could see passengers on board, looking down, wondering what on earth was going on.

I felt my cheeks scorch scarlet as Claire came towards me.

"Everything OK, Mary?" she asked.

"This Rebel Wilson – famous American film star," said Ernesto.

I looked from him to Claire and back again, unsure what to say.

"Well, Rebel has to come on board now," said Claire.

"I will go see new film," shouted Ernesto.

"We all go see Garden Centre in Cobham," said another voice.

"Good luck," they cried, as I followed the incredulous Claire onto the ship.

"Well that sounds like it was an adventurous day," she said. "I hope you had a lovely time in Lisbon and weren't hassled too much by all your fans."

"A lovely day," I replied.

"I'm glad," she said.

And though every fibre of her being must have been dying to ask what on earth was going on, professionalism won the day and she wished me a good evening and a pleasant dinner, and strode off across the ship, the chants from my new fan club, and cries of 'we love Rebel' still audible as she went.

CHAPTER SIX: EN ROUTE TO GIBRALTAR

"Hey Frank, Frank," I said, as I saw my nonagenarian friend after dinner that evening. I raced up to him at such speed that Janette looked genuinely frightened. If Frank could have seen further than the end of his nose I suspect he would have looked frightened too. As it was, he just sat straight-backed, staring into the distance as I ran towards him.

"Hello," I said, warmly. "It's me - Mary."

Ah Mary. I was hearing all about your intriguing day over dinner. Didn't you manage to convince half of Portugal that you were a famous film star?"

"Yes, something like that," I said.

"I don't think it was Mary's fault," said Janette kindly. "I was speaking to the captain earlier. A load of people just decided that she looked like a film star and began running around after her. Not her fault at all."

"Ahhh. Look, don't tell anyone else but it was my fault. The truth is that I told a guy on the tram that I was Rebel Wilson. God knows why...I regretted it as soon as I'd said it. I certainly didn't expect them all to chase around after me and ask for autographs, but it was all definitely my fault. I feel such an idiot. I'm always doing things like that, Frank. Always getting myself into a complete state."

I looked over at Frank and he was smiling broadly, his shoulders shaking slightly as he laughed.

"Always a joy to meet someone who doesn't take life too seriously," he said. "Your generation can be so serious about the most trivial of things. I've never understood why. Go tell 'em you're Rebel whatever her name is if you want to. Tell them you're the Queen of Sheba if you want. Life's supposed to be full of surprises, Mary Brown. Don't let anyone tell you otherwise."

"Yes," I said, with a smile. "And when the psychiatric nurses come to take me away I shall say that it is all your fault."

"Of course," said Frank. "Just blame me. I'm too old to go to jail."

"Can you carry on the story you were telling me earlier. You know...about you going off to war."

Frank laughed to himself. "Are you sure? You don't want to be spending half your time talking to an elderly man."

"I'm fascinated. Please tell me everything. PLEASE."

"OK," said Frank, smiling and shaking his head. "I can't remember where we got to. Did I tell you about Jim and Tom?"

"No. Who were they?"

"OK. Let me take you back to November 1942," he said, his voice soothing and calm. "Close your eyes for a minute and think about it. I was just a teenager and I'd received my call-up and within a few days I was on a military flight to Tunisia. I sat there, in my newly acquired uniform, surrounded by complete strangers. I couldn't believe what was happening. Before that I'd worked on the fish market. I'd never been out of the county."

I adjusted myself in my seat, taking a gulp of gin and tonic and resting my feet on the small, glass coffee table in front of me. I closed my eyes.

"OK, I'm there," I said. "I'm on the plane with you."

"Most of the men on the flight with me were older," he continued. "They had been serving for a couple of years and were being redeployed. I felt like I was the only one going into combat for the first time. I was so much younger and much more inexperienced than the others. It was like they had known a world that I knew nothing of. Then I got chatting to two guys, they were called Tom and Jim. Great guys. Like me, they were off to war for the first time. They were a bit older but not much. Tom was from Birmingham and Jim was from Slough. Very funny and entertaining on the journey out there they were. Full of mischief. I guess it was what you'd call gallows humour...all of us trying to cope with what might lie ahead, but it was humour all the same. We quickly became close friends."

Frank stopped to take a sip of his drink which had been poured into a plastic beaker to make it easier for him. He lifted the bright blue cup with his shaking hand and Janette rushed to help.

"We all arrived safely and I remember walking out into the furnace. I'd never felt heat like it before...this burning, intense heat that seemed to blast itself into us. Then we were taken for a briefing session before being handed weapons and equipment. I'd had a few basic training sessions in England before leaving, but I didn't really know what I was doing. When I look back now...I was just a kid. I knew nothing. Nothing at all.

"I remember one time, after we'd been on the move for a while without seeing anything, we were walking across the sand and we saw a plane overhead. Jim thought it was a German bomber so we all jumped into a ditch nearby. We didn't realise that the ditch was full of stagnant water. Nor did we realise that it was a US plane so there was no need for to have hidden at all. We looked up and all the other soldiers were standing looking down at us. They had more experience; they knew a US plane from a German bomber. My goodness we stank after that...for days and days, because it was hard to wash. God we stank.

"I remember the first people we came across were Arabs sitting on their camels and making their wives walk along by their sides. Tom made the Arabs get off and put the women on the camels! He was a big lad, Tom, you wouldn't argue with him.

"The Arabs were nice guys. We got to know them fairly well before we got into serious combat. We learned to respect the local culture. We struck up friendships with the Bedouin. They were the salt of the earth. They were generous and polite to a fault.

"When we were in camp, though, I felt a bit useless. I was good for carrying things and fetching things, but Tom was a carpenter and Jim was a chef, so they had proper skills. At one point, Tom created this latrine for us that was a work of art. It was 100m from the main tent lines and faced toward the Atlas Mountains. The only trouble was - the loo got used a lot, by a lot of blokes and one day the main supporting beam gave way with a mighty crack, there was a loud howl and Jenkins rushed out with his trousers round his ankles. The whole thing had broken. We were back to using holes in the ground after that, but it had been nice while it lasted.

"Me, Tom and Jim laughed all the time and we went everywhere together, like brothers we were. That was before the fighting started. Do you have any relatives who fought in the war, Mary?"

"No," I said. "No, I haven't."

"Good. I'm glad. War is terrifying. Worse than you can possibly imagine. Don't let anyone tell you otherwise. Don't let puffed up army generals convince you that war is good for anything, don't let politicians who want to make a name for themselves incite conflict. No one who fought of the western front, no one who went through what we went through can look at their medals without weeping. War is messy and solves nothing. Nothing."

There was a pause and I wasn't quite sure what to say. I desperately wanted him to carry on with his story, but didn't feel it was appropriate to hurry him when it was clearly so difficult for him to talk about it.

"Lots of the guys perished, one was right next to me when a bomb blew him to pieces in a second. I saw him explode. Can you imagine what that's like? The noise from the shells and bombs was deafening. Most nights were lit up with gunfire. We were dive bombed and machine gunned by Stukhas, 13 of our lads killed, 10 wounded.

"Jim, Tom and I stayed tight as anything through all this. We'd seen so many people die and been forced to grow up so fast. It helped that we looked out for one another. Then one day we walked to the hills of Tunisia. It was a hellish journey. We joked about there being pretty girls at the top and flagons of ale for everyone.

"Our mission was to capture Longstop Hill. If we succeeded it would open up the road to Tunis. We trudged up the slopes of the hill in blinding rain. All you could hear was "slop ... slop" as each foot was lifted from the mud. There was so much noise from bullets and it was dark and the sheeting rain made it impossible to see anything. You'd hear cries as your colleagues were hit. Many of the wounded sank into the mud and died. The rain and wind muffled the cries of the dying. We got to the top and there was no sign of Jim or Tom. I ran around screaming for them, crying their names but it was no good.

"Then two of the lads appeared carrying Jim, he was badly injured. He'd tried to save Tom but it was no good. Tom had been hit and collapsed into the mud and died. We got Jim to an MDS - that's a Medical Dressing

Station - but it was all too late. He clung on for a few hours then died. He looked me in the eye and said goodbye."

"Oh no," I said. "Oh God - this is awful. You lost two friends on the same night?"

"I did, dear," he said, his voice croaking with pain. "And Jim turned to me as life slipped away from him and said. 'Look after my wife for me won't you Frank. Keep an eye on her. Will you? Please say you will'."

"Of course I will," I said. "Jim, I promise you." Then his eyes closed and he died.

"Frank I can't imagine what it must have been like to lose a friend like that. When I think of my friends and how much they mean to me...it's heart-breaking."

"It was very difficult," he said, staring off into space into an imaginary place that he seemed to escape to so frequently. "I need to go back to see where I lost them...one last time, and to say goodbye properly. Janette will be there with me. It'll mean so much to both of us."

"I suppose you want to go because you've heard all the incredible stores over the years," I said to Janette.

"Yes, and because Jim was my grandfather," she said.

"Oh my God! That's so lovely," I said. "How did you two end up meeting?"

"I kept my promise to Jim. I went and made sure his wife was OK and I got to know his family and helped to look after them."

"Oh, how wonderful," I said, settling into my seat and curling by feet beneath me. "Tell me more."

"Frank's tired now," said Janette, protectively.

"I promise I'll tell you more tomorrow," said Frank, as Janette stood up and prepared to push him away. "I haven't told you about Irene yet. We'll do that story tomorrow."

"Yes, please," I said, shouting after him. "Please tell me all about it tomorrow."

CHAPTER SEVEN: SECOND STOP – GIBRALTAR

Cruising had done something to my internal clock. I went to bed early last night and was up early this morning - most unlike me. As the sun rose I was to be found standing on deck in a large sunhat and dark glasses to watch as we travelled down the south coast of Spain towards the Straits of Gibraltar. It was quite chilly that time of the morning, and not at all bright so the sunhat and glasses were entirely unneeded, but I felt they offered me an appropriate disguise should Simon saunter on to deck. I was astonished that I hadn't bumped into him, but quite sure that a meeting was inevitable, and I had to be on my guard at all times.

I was standing next to a guy called Malcolm as the ship sailed along. He'd been on my table on the first night, a wiry man with a warm, friendly face. He had been talking mainly about politics, so I hadn't really engaged with him all that much. I don't know a great deal about politics: only that Theresa May wears great shoes and Donald Trump is a giant, orange loon-bucket and no one knows how he was elected.

"One of Britain's last remaining colonies," said Malcolm, as we drifted along. I tried to look interested in what he was saying, but it was very hard. "British colonies," he said, shaking his head. I shook mine too because I didn't know what to do.

"How is your friend?" he asked. "Still not well enough to leave the cabin?"

"No, she's going to stay in there for a little bit longer...until she feels stronger."

"Goodness," he said. "How awful for her - missing all of this."

"Yes, absolutely," I said. "I've been telling her all about it."

"Very good. Lots of pictures for her to see?"

"Yes, that's right," I said.

"Would you like to join my wife and me today, as we look around?"

How do you answer a question like that? I absolutely did not want to spend the day with these two. His wife was a wide-eyed woman with mad frizzy hair and the look of a woodland animal that had just emerged into the light. The only thing I'd really learned about the two of them was that they loved talking politics and were frantic about cleanliness and spent their whole time wiping down surfaces. I just didn't think we'd get on at all.

"I'd love to," I said warmly. "Thank you very much for asking."

Then I stomped back to my cabin to get my things, feeling very cross for not being able to think up a reason on the spot why I couldn't go with them. I ate a packet of crisps, an odd-looking chocolate bar that I thought was a Twix but when I bit into it I realised it wasn't (it was horribly runny caramel with bits of nougat and raisins in it, but I ate it anyway), and a packet of peanuts. Then I felt doubly annoyed with myself - first for getting pushed into spending the day with the woodland creatures, then for eating all the snacks in the fridge after just enjoying a massive buffet breakfast. If I carried on eating like this, the damn ship would sink beneath the weight of me.

It was quite an easy walk into town from the port, even for a hugely overweight woman in white Capri pants that were at least two sizes too small (I had bought the size 18s convinced, I mean CONVINCED, that I would lose weight and fit into them but here we were a year later and they were no more able to fit me than they were able to fly to the moon).

We walked along; passing a small statue in the middle of a roundabout which gleamed in the morning sunshine as if was made of fire. It was quite breathtaking.

"Would you mind taking a picture of me?" I asked, reaching out to give my phone to Mary. "It's very straightforward – just an iphone...you press there."

But Edith looked very embarrassed. "I'm sorry, we don't do that," she said. "Germs."

"Don't do what?"

"Touch other people's phones."

"Right, OK," I said, walking over to the statue and preparing to take a selfie. "I'll do it myself. I'm fine with my germs." This day was going as well as I thought it would.

"Don't take offence," she said. "Nothing personal."

But it was hard not to take it personally when someone point blank refused to touch something that belonged to you incase you infected them.

Once I'd got my selfie, we walked across the square to Main Street where there were lots of bars and restaurants.

"Shall we stop for a coffee and work out what to do next?" I said, but I knew what the answer would be.

"A lot of these cafes are quite dirty," said Edith. "And the coffee on the ship is free, let's wait until we get back before we have coffee."

I tried to be understanding, but this was bonkers.

"I might just get one to take away," I said, more to assert myself than because of any overwhelming desire for coffee. It was very much the Malcolm and Edith show, with me just tagging along behind. It was all making me feel very uncomfortable. I would get coffee whether they approved or not.

"Right, where shall we go next?" I said, leaning on the side of the coffee shop and sipping a ridiculously strong, piping hot coffee that I didn't want at all. It was so incredibly hot already. The last thing I needed was coffee with the consistency of gravy. Also, my white trousers were killing me. I'd undone the button so I could breathe, but they still hurt. Edith was wearing tennis shorts and a Fred Perry t-shirt with a sun visor. Her legs were the colour of mashed potato, she looked like she'd never been exposed to the sun ever before, but she looked fresh and comfortable. I found myself wishing I was dressed like her, and I bet no one has ever wished that before.

Edith produced a map and a tourist information leaflet about Gibraltar.

"Right, here we go," she said. "Gibraltar has a population of around 30,000 and is a tiny 2.6 square miles so it's easy to walk round."

I wanted to point out that nowhere was easy to walk around in these trousers but that seemed a bit churlish. I looked down at the map, at where Edith had her finger pushed into our current location...

"We thought we'd just head up the Rock of Gibraltar, walk around and see the wild monkeys," said Edith. "I've brought some food from the buffet for us to have a picnic lunch. I'm not sure we'll have time to do much else before we're due back on the ship."

I longed to come up with an alternative suggestion, just to be awkward - this is what having too-tight trousers does to a woman. But I couldn't think of a better plan, so I acquiesced.

"Yes," I said, following behind them, feeling like an angry teenager. Wishing I hadn't worn the white trousers, wishing it wasn't so hot, and wishing I hadn't eaten so much at breakfast.

Despite all my reservations, Gibraltar was really good fun in the end. Edith and Malcolm were nice people.

Their obsession with cleanliness was bordering on insanity, but I learned to see the funny side, and mocked them gently as they wiped everything down and spritzed their hands constantly. Most importantly, I saw the monkeys - the best bit by far. They were everywhere...everywhere - scampering around the place, not like the big baboons I'd encountered on safari and which had left me terrified and climbing a tree to escape - these were friendly, perky little things. I loved them. I loved them so much that I didn't want to leave them, so I stayed and had the picnic lunch instead of heading for a restaurant as I'd planned to. While we dined on bread, cheese, crisps and dips, I told them all about Frank.

"What an incredible story. I have to say we've really enjoyed spending the day with you," said Edith, as she attempted to pack away the remains of the picnic while I tried to eat it from out of her hands as she did so.

"Thank you for having me," I said, trying to take a handful of crisps from the bowl as she put them into a carrier bag for disposal. "It's been nice to get to know you."

"Right, enough of this, back to the ship," said Malcolm, standing up and offering me his hand. I knew that if I took the hand to help me up, I would pull Malcolm down on top of me, so I was forced to pretend I hadn't seen it, then roll onto my side and clamber to my feet.

"Let's go," I said, charging onwards towards our floating hotel.

CHAPTER EIGHT: CAPTURED BY THE GERMANS

"Hello sir, what a pleasure," I said to Frank, as I took my seat next to him at dinner that evening. I'd explained to the captain that Dawn had a terrible migraine so would stay in the room. He'd offered to send someone in to check on her, but – as usual – I reassured him that she just needed to rest and that she would be much better off if we all left her alone.

"Such a shame that your friend is unwell," said Frank.

"If I tell you a secret, will you promise to carry on with your story over dinner," I whispered.

"Oh, how intriguing," he replied. "Of course."

"Well, Dawn's not actually with me on the ship, but she doesn't want me to tell people that she's not here, so I'm kind of just saying that she's ill all the time. It's bloody nuts."

"Ha, ha," said Frank, with a smile. "Lots of very 'nuts things' seem to happen around you. I like it!"

"All well," said voices behind me. It was Malcolm and Edith. "I hope you don't mind us intruding, but Edith wanted to meet Frank," said Malcolm. "We loved your story about him earlier."

I made the introductions and explained to Frank that I'd been telling them about him.

"Frank's about to carry on with his story, aren't you, Frank?"

"May we stay and listen?" asked Malcolm and Edith in unison, taking a seat at our table. "Is that OK?"

"Of course," said Frank. "If you want, but I'm sure there must be other things you want to talk about."

"No, no. We want to hear about the war," I said, and then I turned to Malcolm and Edith: "So - just to recap - he lost his two great friends - Tom and Jim - in Tunisia while trying to capture Longstop Hill. Now - what happened next?"

"My, my, you've been listening," said Frank. "That's cheering for an old man to hear."

"Of course I've been listening," I said. "It's amazing."

"Well I suppose I'd better carry on then, hadn't I? OK, well we managed to capture the hill position and the British army marched into Tunisia...it was a very special, very important victory, but I was numb. I felt that nothing in my life would ever be the same again, and in many ways I was right...it wasn't.

"Everything felt flat and colourless after that. Nothing had quite the same meaning for those days, weeks and months after I lost my friends.

"The battalion headed for Sicily after Tunisia and I went with them, feeling weary and worldlier than I should have been at that tender age. The seventh and eighth Army combined forces and headed through Sicily towards Corleone. The joining of two battalions meant we weren't being properly led - officers vied for position and the whole thing was a bit of a shambles. The lack of proper leadership came to a head one day when we came up to a river and no one really knew what they were doing. While we were waiting to cross it, some of us were captured by the Germans."

"Oh no," I said. "After you'd been through so much."

"Well, yes, and because I had been through so much, I just didn't care anymore. We were rounded up and put into an army vehicle and all I could do was to hope that my death would not be too painful. Nothing mattered, nothing at all. Then one of the lads nudged me. "Follow me," he said. He'd seen a gap that we could escape through so we all filed out.

"But as we were making our escape, the Germans saw us and it was mayhem - we all ran off in different directions. I ran down an alleyway and straight into a Sicilian man standing by his car at the front of a small, white cottage. I looked at him, desperation sweeping through my eyes, as the sound of German voices filled the streets behind us. He hid me behind his small garden wall and stood over me; that man was Antonio Cantania, and he saved my life. "The Germans took a cursory look but when they found no one there, they gave up and left. I told Antonio that I would never be able to thank him enough, and then he invited me back to his house.

"Come, have food," he said. "My daughter will tend to your injuries."

"I looked down to see I was bleeding all down my arm. I had no idea what I'd done or how I'd done it.

Once we got into his house, he called for his daughter. I stood in the hallway, desperate not to drip blood on the polished wooden floors, when I heard footsteps on the stairs. I looked up and I saw her...the most beautiful woman I'd ever seen. Irene. She looked like a movie star. Like Sophia Lauren. Have you heard of her?"

"No," I said. The name wasn't even familiar.

"Look her up," said Frank. "A beautiful Italian actress who was the spitting image of my Irene.

I stopped in my tracks when I saw her and wiped my dirty hand against my trousers before shaking her's. She had these tiny hands, so soft and delicate. "Hello, I'm Irene Cantania," she said, in her lovely Italian accent. For the first time since I'd lost Jim and Tom I actually felt something. Like life wasn't pointless after all. Like there was someone here who moved me, who mattered to me."

"Oh, that's lovely," I said. "Really lovely."

"Beautiful," chorused Malcolm and Edith.

"It was," said Frank. "It was very lovely, and very beautiful, but it was also quite complicated because she had a brother - Alberto - who'd fought with the Germans against us Brits, and although Italy had changed sides, and were fighting with us against the Germans by the time I got there, it was tough."

"What do you mean - Italy changed sides - is that true, or are you joking?"

"No, that's true. Didn't you know that?"

"Er...no," I said.

"They changed sides just months before I arrived at the house. It was very difficult. Her brother had fought against us, and had lost good friends to Allied guns.

British soldiers had killed people in Alberto's battalion. How was he supposed to welcome me into his home?

"There was hostility and anger bubbling away, and real resentment towards me from him and his friends. I wouldn't have stayed more than one night because it was awkward and I knew I shouldn't be there...I should be back with my guys but I was quite badly injured, so stayed longer.

"And I wasn't in any rush to leave because I had fallen hopelessly in love with Irene and I knew that Marco Vellus, a local boy, wanted to marry her. I was determined that before I left I would make her mine. Marco was a friend of her brother's...the whole family assumed they would get married. It was very difficult. But all I cared about was that in the middle of it all was me and Irene - two people who fell for one another despite all the difficulties. We couldn't help ourselves.

"We got on so well. It wasn't like it is now - we didn't jump into bed together or do anything other than sit and chat, but it was enough for me to know that she was the woman I wanted to marry.

"Irene was tending to me daily - my left arm had slivers of shrapnel in it that are still there today and I had badly cut my face, arm and leg. Her father was as kind as he could be, but he knew my presence was tearing his family apart. He told me that I needed to leave. I nodded, thanked him for everything he had done, shook his hand and told him I would leave that night.

"I left, under the cover of darkness, heading towards Salerno where my battalion was based. I swore to Irene that I would be back soon, and we would marry and I would give her the life she deserved. She cried when I left and begged me to come back soon.

"When I left that night I felt like I had something to fight for, something that was worth staying alive for. I headed for Salerno to rejoin my battalion feeling like a different person from the one who'd left Tunisia just weeks earlier. I'd been devastated by the death of my two friends and was feeling helpless and hopeless. Now I felt desperately sad about the loss of my friends, but in their name, and for Irene, I would fight on. There was so much that I wanted to live for. For the first time in my young life I was in love."

CHAPTER NINE: LIFE IN A POW CAMP

"Can I interrupt," said Captain Homarus, leaning over and making sure that my glass was full of wine. "You do know that you have a fan on the boat, don't you?"

"A fan?" I said, scrunching up my face in disbelief.

"Yes. A guy called Simon," he said you used to go out together and you became very ill and moved away. He hasn't seen you for 10 years and now you're back, looking lovelier than ever."

"Oh God, no. To be honest, I've kind of been trying to avoid him."

"Oh," said the captain, tapping the side of his nose. "I'll tell him I haven't seen you then."

"Thank you," I said. "That's really kind of you. The relationship ended because we weren't really suited."

"And because you were seriously ill, according to him."

"Yes, sort of."

"Who's that?" asked Frank.

"Oh, there's this guy on the ship who I went out with years and years ago. It's so embarrassing, he's turned up on the ship and keeps trying to talk to me."

Then I whispered: "To be honest, we used to go out together and I wanted to get rid of him. I told him I had leprosy, isn't that awful? Now he's wondering how on earth I recovered so well."

Frank roared with laughter, while the others looked on, startled by the strange noise he'd just made.

"I'm trying to avoid him but I'm bound to bump into him at some stage."

Frank smiled at me while I spoke. "I'm sure you'll be able to talk your way out of it," he said.

"I'm not so sure," I said. "But enough about me and my stupid mouth. Tell me about you. What happened next?"

"Well, the story takes a bit of a sad turn," said Frank.

"No," we all chorused. I'd forgotten that Edith and Malcolm were still sitting there. They were leaning in, with their elbows on the table and their faces in their hands, like little children listening to a bedtime story.

"Blimey - really? It gets sadder?" I said. "This is already the saddest story I've ever heard."

"I never made it back to my battalion," said Frank. "I was captured again before I reached them. If I had got there, I would have seen there was a letter for me saying that both my parents had been killed. Their lives taken from them in a moment when a bomb dropped on Portsmouth and destroyed our house."

"Oh no, I'm so sorry."

"I wasn't the only one who this happened to...when you go away to war you assume you're the one in danger, but there was as much danger for those left behind, and many soldiers returned home, thinking the worst of the war was behind them, only to discover that family back home hadn't been as lucky.

"Anyway, as I said, I didn't know about this at the time, because before I could make it to Salerno I was captured again but this time there was no escape - and I was sent to Poland to a Prisoner of War camp called Stalag 8a."

"Oh no, how awful. Why Poland? Were they on the German side?"

"No, far from it - they had been occupied by the Germans. The Nazis controlled the country at the time so took prisoners of war there."

I'd read about POW camps at school. I remembered that they sounded like hell on earth.

"What's got everyone so animated," said Captain Homarus, pulling up a chair next to us.

"Frank is telling us about his time in the war. He was captured by the Germans and sent to a Prisoner of War camp."

"Goodness, Frank. How fascinating. Mind if I listen in?"

"Of course," said Frank, smiling to himself as his entourage grew.

"Conditions were tough, rations were meagre. It was hard work," he said. "Doing heavy labour while you were weak from hunger was very difficult. You see images in every war film of men escaping from prison camps, but the truth is that everyone was much too exhausted to escape, and those who got beyond the wire ran the very real risk of being shot. Escape never felt like an option.

"You're so weakened when you're locked up like that. The Germans didn't heat our cells and it was freezing. Night times were difficult. You got to the stage where you'd wake up so cold you were glad just to be alive.

"Daytime wasn't much fun either, I have to tell you – surviving on a daily ration of hot water and barley porridge is tough. I was so skinny. There was nothing of me. It was a horrible, dark, difficult time in which I became convinced every day that I would die.

"I stayed in the camp until the end of the war when we were rescued by Russians. It was May 1945. I've had a great fondness for Russians ever since. I was weak and dirty, cold and hungry and they looked after me. I was taken back to Italy and reunited with my battalion. That's when I was told about the death of my parents."

"Oh Frank," said Captain Homarus. "Your parents were killed in the war?"

"Yes, they were," said Malcolm.

"As soon as I was strong enough, I went to collect Irene – the woman who had kept me sane as I'd been starved, beaten and freezing in the POW camp. I planned to propose to her and take her back to England."

"Ah, good news at last," said Edith. But Frank was looking down at his hands.

"When I got to Sicily I discovered that she was engaged to Marco," he said.

"Noooooo," we all chorused.

"Blimey, Frank, when are you going to get a break? This is insane," I said. "Please tell me that's a joke....I can't bear it."

"No, not a joke...far from a joke," he said.

"Frank needs to go to bed now," said Jan."He needs to get a good night's sleep, tomorrow he will be going to Tunisia to say goodbye to Tom and my grandpa."

We all looked at one another, bereft that the story had to end at this point.

"Just a little bit more," I tried.

"Not tonight," said Janette, and she stood and began pushing Frank away.

"Good luck tomorrow," I shouted, and I saw him nod, as she pushed him away through the dining room and out of view.

CHAPTER TEN: DRAMA IN THE THEATRE

I watched Frank and Janette go, as Captain Homarus went back to work and Edith and Malcolm headed off to bed. I thought about everything he had said. It was hard to imagine what he had been through...what traumas and difficulties he must have endured. It was kind of weird that someone alive today had been through all that. His experiences felt like they should be trapped in the pages of a history book, not living in the memory of that lovely, softly-spoken man.

I left the table and wandered through to the bar area. It was very busy, and getting busier all time, with couples in their finery coming in after dinner, and groups of newly-established friends gathering at tables. I didn't feel like going back to the cabin just yet, so I took a seat on a bar stool.

"Everything OK, Madam," said one of the crew, seeing me sitting alone.

"Yes, I'm fine," I said.

"Can I get you anything? A drink?"

"I'll have a gin and tonic please," I said. I didn't particularly want a drink, but turning one down was beyond me.

The waiter brought me my drink and I suddenly felt quite lonely, and a little lost. I seemed to be the only person sitting on my own. I'm usually really good at making friends but it felt like everyone else was in a couple, and quite settled in their own company. It didn't feel like I could go charging up to them, introduce myself and sit down. I sipped my drink and decided I should walk around for a bit, and then I'd head to bed.

I wandered through the small art shop where people were browsing and commenting on the art and how much they liked it. The only thing that stood out to me was a bronze sculpture of a ballerina. I thought it would look nice in my flat. I turned it over in my hands; it was cool and heavy. The price tag underneath said £3600. Whaaaat? Who would pay that for a sculpture? I wouldn't pay that much for a car.

How did these people have so much money? Where did they make it? I walked out of the shop and past the pub which was playing some sports match that had everyone cheering wildly.

Next to the pub was a small theatre that I'd seen earlier in the day. It looked prettier at night, all lit up and with people all dressed up, sipping champagne in the boxes and settling down to watch a play. I quite fancied going in, but I didn't want to see some desperately dull play by some worthy, philosophical type – I just wasn't in the mood.

"What's on tonight?" I asked the guy on the door.

"It' a medley of songs and dance routines...just a load of fun," he said.

"Oh, that sounds perfect. Do I need a ticket or anything? Or can I just come in?"

"Just come in...you're more than welcome," he said. "Take a seat anywhere. It starts in five minutes."

I settled myself into a seat by the gangway and sipped my gin while waiting for the curtain to go up. People were continuing to come into the theatre and the gentle murmur of voices soothed me as I sat there in quiet contemplation. I couldn't remember the last time I felt so relaxed.

The lights began to dim and I looked round to see how full the theatre was....and that's when I saw him. Shit! Striding into the theatre alone, dressed up to the nines in his tuxedo...Simon. Oh my fucking God. It was definitely him...there was no doubt about it. I recognised the way he pushed one hand deep into his pocket as he walked. The slightly mechanical movements...like he was being controlled by a giant puppet master. There was always something so unnatural about him. I dropped my head so he wouldn't see me, and sunk down in my seat. There was no way I could leave without him seeing me, but – at the same time – there was every chance of him seeing me if I stayed where I was. I had no idea what to do.

I glanced over to see where he was sitting, and I'm sure he saw me. He did a dramatic double-take just as the lights went down. Christ, what now? There was a door to the right of me that was marked 'authorised personnel only'. Under the cover of darkness, I sneaked out of my seat and peeled the door open, sneaking through it into a corridor full of dancers. Honestly, there were dancers everywhere, dressed up in fabulous sequined leotards and feather headdresses.

"You're not dressed," said a man in a tight blue catsuit. "What the hell?"

"I know. I'm late," I said, shuffling from foot to foot, afraid to announce that I wasn't in the cast at all incase he made me go back through the door.

"Damian....one of the larger dancers here needs dressing," said the man, wiggling off towards the stage, while two wardrobe assistants grabbed me and began undressing me. There was a great deal of sighing and muttering as they surveyed the racks of clothes for something for me to wear. I tried to insist that I could just sit in the dressing room and didn't have to be dressed up at all, but this clearly wasn't an option.

"With four dancers ill we need everyone we can find on stage tonight."

"Right, OK," I said, as they wrapped me in blue sequined robes and pinned my hair up, attaching feathers and jewels. It looked quite good by the time they'd finished. So good, in fact, that I completely forgot that there was no way I could go anywhere near the stage for the simple reasons that: (a) I couldn't dance and (b) I didn't know any of the choreography.

"This way," he called.

I could hear that the performance had begun, with loud, music hall songs being belted out on the stage, and the sound of footsteps as the dancers tap danced through their routines.

"You're on next," said a behind-the-scenes assistant, leading me through to the edge of the stage. The headdress was so bloody heavy. I had no idea how I was supposed to dance in it.

"Good luck," said the guy, pulling back the curtain a little for me to go on. "When they sing 'arimbo, arimbo' that's when you pull off your top to reveal your tasselled nipples."

"That's when I what?" I said, regarding him with a mixture of alarm and confusion.

"Go!" he said. I strode onto the stage, trying to keep my head upright so the damn headdress wouldn't come tumbling off, and trying to do some sort of steps that could be described as being in any way dance-like. The guy in the blue catsuit looked at me like I was insane as I danced around on the spot, clicking my fingers and stamping my feet, while all the other dancers moved together in a lovely rhythmical dance that they had clearly been practising for months and which I could in no way hope to pick up.

Then, it happened. "Ariba, Ariba!" came the shout, and four of the dancers pulled off their tops. I just looked at them...wide mouthed and disbelieving. I turned out towards the crowd and saw Simon. His eye caught mine and he stood up.

"Oh my God – Mary Brown – it's you. It's a miracle!" he shouted. "I thought you were dying of leprosy."

"No, I'm better," I shouted back, as the headdress slipped over my eyes. "The leprosy has all gone."

CHAPTER ELEVEN: GYM BUDDIES

I woke early the next morning and stretched out across the bed. It was so comfortable I didn't want to move. The sun was streaming in through the balcony windows where I'd forgotten to close the curtains again. I looked out across the white pillow, towards the ocean, then I saw it – a bright blue feather lying next to me along with a sprinkling of glitter – and all the horrors of the night before came bounding back to me.

Juan Pedro, the head dancer, had been hysterical afterwards – laughing uproariously when I told him of my conundrum and that I wasn't a dancer at all.

"No! Really? I couldn't tell," he said, mimicking my little solo dance routine and the look of fear on my face when he'd shouted 'Ariba.'

"I particularly liked the stamping," he'd said, and the way your eyes moved upwards towards the headdress all the time because you were sure it was going to fall off.

"It's hard work," I'd said. "Dancing and holding the weight of that thing on your head...I have a whole new respect for dancers."

I'd told him all about Simon and my efforts to avoid him, and he laughed a lot at the fact that, far from managing to avoid Simon and keep the whole thing quiet, I'd been forced to address it in a packed theatre and announce from the stage, while dressed in glitter and feathers, that I used to have leprosy.

"You must see the funny side," he insisted. I wasn't sure that I did, but I was confident that everyone else would.

Now it was morning and my head hurt and it was only 6am. There was no way I was going to get back to sleep, so I climbed out of bed and made the unprecedented decision to go up to the gym and do a workout before breakfast. There was a 'wake up workout' session taking place at 6.30am. If I did that, I could then justify going completely nuts at the buffet later. So, off I went up onto the top deck to find the work out class.

I walked into the glass panelled room to find Juan Pedro sitting there, legs akimbo, stretching out.

"Ah, you're doing this class as well are you?" I asked.

"I'm taking this class, darling," he replied. "I hope you're ready to work hard."

"No, not really," I said. "Especially not after last night's extravagances."

"It'll do you good...it'll help get the booze out of your system. Also, I hear it helps to do lots of exercise if you've suffered from leprosy."

"Stop it," I said, nudging him playfully.

There were six people in the class – three of them were dancers from last night – lithe, slim and gorgeous young men, the other two were called Bob and Doris and looked about 75. I fancied my chances of being more able than the elderly couple, but considerably less able than the dancers.

The music struck up – loud drum beats that rocked through me, making my hangover feel instantly about five times worse.

"OK, and marching on the spot," said Juan Pedro. "Lift your knees as high as possible, come on, I want to see those knees up by your shoulders."

I did the best I could, though I have to report that my knees were nowhere near my shoulders. Still, I had a light sweat and found I was quite enjoying it. That's when Juan Pedro put down steps in front of us and said that for the second half of the class we'd do a step routine.

He had us stepping on and off the steps at high speed, kicking out and lifting her arms.

"Don't worry if you get lost – just keep going," he said, in an encouraging voice, so I gleefully stepped on and off the step, waving my arms, completely out of time with everyone else in the class.

Afterwards Juan Pedro came up to me and put his arm around me.

"Well done," he said. "You kept going all the way through."

"Thanks," I said. I was proud of myself too. I can't remember the last time I did an exercise class like that and kept going. "I really want to try and lose weight, but it's so hard when you love food."

"Yes, and these ships are a menace, with all those buffets," he said. "They're impossible to resist."

He tapped his rock hard, not-an-ounce-of-fat-stomach as he spoke, as if to illustrate how much weight he'd put on.

"There's nothing there," I said, rubbing my own stomach and seeing how it rippled wildly like it was a separate entity entirely. Like a man made of jelly was lying on my tummy.

"You keep up the exercise and that will go in no time," said Juan Pedro. "You just need to cut back on the food a little, and exercise a bit more – it's not rocket science...none of it is difficult, you just need to make a promise to yourself to take your health seriously from now on."

"I think I will," I said, standing up, and wiping the sweat from my brow.

"Good," said Juan Pedro. "Fancy breakfast?"

Going down to breakfast with Juan Pedro was great, and it made me realised how much I don't like being on my own...how much I like to have company. I live on my own, but I'm at work a lot of the time and when I'm not, I either have Ted round or I'm at his. Or I'm out with friends. I never spend a lot of time alone.

The only downside to going to breakfast with Juan Pedro, was having to be so restrained. Having had a conversation with him about how I wanted to lose weight, it felt all wrong to pile my plate high with pancakes, syrup and croissants. But – and this is the thing that people don't understand about fat people – I can't not have those things. If I don't have a pancake and syrup at breakfast I'll feel awful and deeply deprived all day and it will play on my mind until I cave in and go to a sweet shop and eat everything they've got.

I ended up walking to the buffet, piling my bowl with melon and pineapple, then shoving a couple of pancakes into my mouth while still there, so Juan Pedro wouldn't be able to see.

I grabbed a pancake, lay it on my hand and dribbled maple syrup into it, before rolling it up and pushing it into my mouth...all while pretending just to eat fruit. I grabbed another pancake and this time laid bacon into it and loads of maple syrup – I shoved the whole thing into my mouth. Then I walked back to my seat with my little bowl of fresh fruit salad.

"Well done," said Juan Pedro, looking at the food I'd selected. "That's brilliant. It can be so hard to eat sensibly with so many unhealthy options on offer. That's really good."

So I ate the lousy pieces of pineapple and melon and took his praise on board. "Thank you, Juan Pedro," I said, the taste of delicious pancakes and maple syrup still strong in my mouth. "Thank you."

"Listen, do you fancy spending the day together in Tunisia? Walking round on your own won't be much fun."

"That would be lovely," I said. "If you don't mind..."

"Mind? I'd love that. Any woman who will rock up and join a dance troupe with no dancing experience in order to escape from a boyfriend who she told she had leprosy is my kind of woman. Especially if that woman then proceeds to stuff her face with pancakes and pretend only to eat two small slivers of melon for breakfast. Perfect."

CHAPTER TWELVE: DRESSED UP IN TUNISIA

I'd arranged to meet Juan Pedro on deck so we could head into Tunis together and explore the sights. I didn't know quite what to expect, but he was good fun and - much as I loved Frank's stories of wartime love and loss - it would be good to have a light-hearted day of fun and frolics with a nutter like Juan Pedro.

"Coming then?" he said, appearing beside me in an odd, but strangely flattering, clothing combo - skin-tight jeans that were ripped both at the knee and alarmingly close to his crotch, along with a shirt with ruffles down the front of it and a very fancy, patterned, shiny blazer. His hair was combed back.

"Glad you made an effort," I said.

"Well, I'm glad one of us did," he retorted, looking me up and down.

"Cheeky hound. It's not easy to be glamorous when you're 19 stone."

Juan Pedro laughed. "You're not 19 stone," he said.

Actually, I am. But I didn't want to push the point, so I decided to take it as a compliment and smiled at him.

"I bet I could get you a fabulous outfit today," he said. "I could make you look gorgeous."

Now, dear readers, I should have realised that this wasn't going to end well. You only had to look at Juan and his bright, shiny blazer and skin-tight, ripped jeans to see that his idea of 'glamorous' was going to be entirely different from mine. I wanted to look like Grace Kelly, he was clearly going to dress me like Danny Le Rue. But all of those thoughts didn't enter my head. All I heard was 'I can make you look gorgeous' and I thought 'I'd like that,' so off we went, into Tunis, with Juan talking about the lovely, native dress, and describing something called a sefsari - a gorgeous huge scarf he wanted to buy for me. He told me about dresses lined with rhinestones. "A gorgeous bodice studded with crystals would be wonderful," he said.

"Bodice? Have you seen the size of my breasts?" I replied. "There aren't enough crystals in the entire world..."

We decided that a stop in a lovely Turkish cafe was called for, before we began our shopping expedition, so we wandered into the first one we came to and ordered drinks.

"Not too strong," I said, as Juan Pedro raised his eyebrows. "You might be in the wrong place altogether if you want weak coffee, doll," he said. "They take it strong and dark here."

The coffee came. As predicted – tiny cups full of wildly strong coffee that was undrinkable.

"Mmmm..." I said. "Mary loves hot tar in the mornings."

There was an added bonus with the coffee when I stirred it because it had this sludge at the bottom – like the sort of stuff you get on the floor of a river bed.

"Fancy another?" said Juan.

I pushed my cup over to him. "Have mine," I said. "I can't do it. The taste of it is making me want to cry."

I looked on the map as we talked. I'm a terrible map reader, but hoped to see roughly where the town centre was. As I scanned across it I saw a sign for Longstop Hill.

"That's where Frank's going," I said, pointing it out. "You know Frank – the old guy on the ship...in the wheelchair...he fought there in the war and two of his friends died. He's going back to say a final goodbye to them."

"Really?" said Juan. "I know all about the battle of Longstop Hill."

"No you don't." It seemed very unlikely that Juan Pedro would know anything at all about battles fought in the Second World War

"I do," he insisted. "It was a crucial battle. When they took control of the hill they were able to go straight into Tunis."

"Yes, that's right. That's what Frank said." I looked at Juan, amazed.

"I took a group of vets out there. They had fought there too and wanted to go back to see it," he explained.

"Gosh, you must tell Frank tonight," I said. "He'd love to hear that."

"Of course," said Juan. "How interesting that he's come back to see it too. It sounds like it was hell up there. The guys I took up had lost friends – they were hit and fell and died in the mud."

"That's what Frank said. That's how he lost one of his friends, the other one died just after they got him to safety."

"Awful," said Juan. "You couldn't imagine any of that if you look at the hill now. It's grassy and pleasant, with goats roaming over it. There is a new road through the Kasserine Pass – the only sign of the war is when it runs past the rusted ruins of tanks. Farmers find shattered helmets in the fields occasionally, but that's it. There's no doubt though – the landings in North Africa and the Tunisian campaign were vital in the final surrender of the Germans. Frank played an important role in securing our freedom today."

There was a moment of solemnity as we both looked down in quiet contemplation, then Juan spoke: "So, shall we use that hard-won freedom by going shopping?"

"Yes," I said. "Let's go shop."

We pushed our chairs back from the table and Juan leaned over to touch my arm. "One condition," he said. "Whatever outfit we buy for you this afternoon, you have to wear at the dinner this evening."

"Done," I said, with staggering naivety, and we wandered off, arm in arm to the shops of downtown Tunisia.

CHAPTER THIRTEEN: THE FINAL PART OF THE STORY

"No, "he said. "Go back and put the gold chains on."

"But I look ridiculous with this much jewellery. "

"No – you look very glamorous with this much jewellery. "

I walked back into the changing room and looked at myself in the mirror. My arms were full of gold bangles, I had a dress on which was deep pink cotton on the top and had puffy sleeves and a fitted bodice which fell from the waist into a skirt shot through with gold thread. Over my head I had a pink scarf studded with crystals and gold necklaces were tied around my forehead with these gold discs dangling down. I had similar necklaces around my neck...lots of them. My upper body was so heavy I could barely stand straight.

Juan was unperturbed by the pain I was in. "No pain no gain," he said. "You have to suffer for your art. It looks really good; I don't see what the problem is. "

I looked back into the mirror. "You don't see what the problem is? I look like a gypsy."

"You don't look like a gypsy, look like a very glamorous Tunisian woman. Trust me," he said. "When you wear this to dinner tonight everybody will think it's amazing."

"I'm not wearing this to dinner tonight, absolutely no way," I said.

"That was the deal," said Juan. "You promised me that if I got you into a glamorous outfit you would wear it for dinner tonight. "

"Yes, but I didn't realise I took so bloody ridiculous."

"You don't. You look glamorous and gorgeous and you're wearing this tonight."

To say that people looked at me with shock in their eyes when I walked into dinner, back on the ship that evening, would be to understate the impact I had. Elegant women wandered all around in black column dresses, cream sun dresses and stylish party dresses, and in the middle of it all was me - a woman of nearly 20 stone dressed head to foot in pink with huge gold jewellery dripping from everywhere. I had more jewellery on me then everybody else on the ship combined, and there were a lot of women with a lot of jewellery on.

I'd had a gin and tonic in the cabin to take the edge off it, but the edges were still very much there as I walked onto the dining floor and I caught up with Juan who continued to say how great I looked.

In front of us I could see Frank, sitting alone at a table with Janette. I desperately need to talk to someone non judgemental, so headed over there, dragging Juan with me, and telling him he needed to meet Frank so they could talk about Longstop Hill.

"Good evening," I said.

Janet jumped when she saw me.

"I thought you were an exotic dancer then," she said. "I thought you were going to give Frank a heart attack."

"No, it's just me. And this is Juan," I said, jangling as I made the introductions. "He dragged me round Turkish boutiques today, telling me he'd make me look me glamorous, but I feel like a complete idiot."

"You don't look like an idiot at all. You look beautiful," said Frank.

"Thank you," I said. The fact that he was almost blind made his compliments less reassuring, but it was kind all the same. "How was Longstop Hill today?"

"Moving," said Frank, nodding his head. "It was very moving. Quite difficult at times, but I'm very glad I did it."

"I found it moving too, and I never fought anyone or anything in my whole life," said Juan.

"You were there today?" said Frank.

"No, I went a few weeks ago. I took a group of Vets. They said the same. Very difficult but very, very worthwhile."

"Yes, the memories have never faded, so it wasn't like I went there and the memories suddenly came pouring back, but being there did cut through me a bit, made me think of all those brave young men who died. That was very difficult."

Janette and I sat and listened awhile while Frank talked through the day. I jingled and jangled every time I nodded my agreement, and Janette looked at me sternly as if my musical accompaniments were somehow lessening the impact of the story.

"Listen, it's incredible to meet you Frank, but I'm going to have to head off to dance practice. We've got a show later. Will you come?"

"I won't. I'm exhausted after the trip today, but thank you for asking. Good luck!"

"Thank you," said Juan, blowing me a kiss as he walked away.

"He seems like a nice young man. Is he your boyfriend?" asked Frank.

"Er...no, I'm pretty sure he's gay," I replied. "Anyway, he wouldn't be my boyfriend if he was the straightest man in the world. He's made me look a complete fool. I'm dressed like a gypsy thanks to him."

Frank just smiled and shook his head. "I bet you look adorable."

"I look like mad gypsy Rose-Lee. People will be asking me to read their fortunes."

Over dinner that evening, Frank and I resumed our chat, with Frank picking up where he'd left off...arriving in Sicily to discover that Irene was engaged.

"I felt as if my insides had been churned out," he said. "I didn't even try to see Irene, as soon as I heard the news, I turned and walked away."

"No! Why didn't you try and find her and persuade her? She probably got engaged to him because she thought you weren't coming back...you were away so long. How could you just walk away?"

"I didn't want to spoil her happiness, if she chose him, then who was I to ruin it for them? Remember, her father had saved my life and her family had been incredibly kind to me. I didn't want to make life difficult for them at all. I just turned and walked away."

"And what did you do then? Where did you go?"

"I left and got the boat back to England but I couldn't stop thinking about her. I got home and that's when I realised how much she mattered. Nothing was there, my family had been wiped out, and the house was boarded up. I was offered temporary accommodation but decided, instead, to travel to Slough to fulfil my friend's dying wish to take care of his wife."

I noticed Janette smiling as Frank spoke about Jim's wife.

"It was lovely to meet her. What a charming lady. Elizabeth was her name. She was standing there with a little three-year-old girl called Linda at her feet."

"Linda was my mum," said Janette. "Dad never found out that mum was pregnant. He never knew he had a daughter."

"Oh no, that's really sad," I said.

"It was a difficult time for mum, but Frank really looked after them. He moved them into his mum's old house as soon as that was repaired and took care of them."

"And your grandma really helped me too," said Frank. "It was Elizabeth who forced me to go to Sicily and try to win back Irene's heart.

"I got a boat back a week later and talked to Irene. She was astonished to see me. I'd been away so long;

she assumed I'd been killed. We talked for hours and I told her I loved her. She said she loved me too, and we hatched a plan to run away together. It wasn't a brave thing to do and it wasn't fair on this family who'd cared so much for me, but we ran away in the night, leaving a note for her parents and one for Marco.

"We settled in England and she never went back. I know she missed her home and her family. She wrote to her parents and went over to visit them secretly, but never saw her brother ever again because she was worried he would come over to England and find me if he knew where we were.

"I need to go back to the house in Sicily to see who is there and to say sorry for everything that happened. Those guys saved my life. They were kind, decent people. I need to see them once more, just to say I'm sorry about the way I took their daughter away from them. Even if everyone I knew is dead, I want to say sorry to anyone there who knew Irene and explain why we ran away; explain to Alberto why she never stayed in touch.

"She wrote letters to Alberto and I thought she was sending them, but after her death I found them in a vanity case; she'd not sent them because she was worried he'd come and find her."

"Gosh, what does Irene think about you going?" I asked.

"Irene died four months ago. She'd been very ill. She passed away peacefully. I'm hopelessly lost without her. I miss her terribly. I need to do this for her. I do hope we find the cottage. We will, won't we?" he said.

"We will. I promise we will," I said. And suddenly I realised that I would be going with him in Sicily and that I absolutely had to help him find Irene's relatives.

CHAPTER FOURTEEN: JUAN'S COMING TOO

I didn't see Frank much over the next couple of days, after hearing the rest of his emotional story on the boat. His journey to Longstop Hill had exhausted him so he stayed on board, mainly in his cabin, being looked after Janette, while the boat stopped first in Sardinia, then in Malta. I explored them both with Juan Pedro. But I couldn't stop thinking about Frank's tale.

"Hey Juan Pedro," I said, as we both sat there, sunning ourselves on the deck one day. "You know Frank – the old guy in the wheelchair who went to Longstop Hill?"

"Yeah," he said, without moving his tanned face from its position, staring up into the sunshine. "Nice guy. I liked him."

"I'm going with him for the day when we get to Sicily - he's going to try and find the cottage that his wife lived in when he first met her. He stole her away from her fiancé just after the war. He wants to go back there and - kind of - make amends to anyone who's still there. He still feels bad that Irene was forced to abandon her family."

"Blimey doll. I doubt there'd be anyone there now that was alive then."

"Well, Frank's still alive, so there could be."

"True darling," said Juan. "I suppose it's worth him trying."

"Did you hear about the letters he has...letters that Irene wrote to her brother to explain why she'd left and updating him on her life and what was going on. She wrote hundreds and never sent any of them. After she died he found the letters in her vanity case with a note saying 'Frank, I'm sorry - I never sent these - I was worried about Marco finding our address and coming to hurt you. I'm sorry'."

"Good grief doll, said Juan, turning himself slightly so he faced the sun. "We're in the middle of a Sunday afternoon rom-com; you know that, don't you? Hugh Grant is going to show up any moment."

"Ha ha. Very funny. It does seem like that. I've been writing all about it in the blog I'm doing for Dawn and apparently it's got quite a big following back home...loads of comments and tonnes of likes."

"My God. They are definitely going to make this into a film. We'll get back to Southampton and there'll be a film crew and director waiting there. Who's going to play us? I was thinking maybe Johnny Depp for me and Jennifer Lawrence for you. What do you think?"

"Yep, I'll go with that," I said. "It would make a brilliant film - Frank's story is so amazing...I just love him. I think he's one of the kindest, warmest and most friendly people ever. Considering what he's been through, you think he'd be wary and guarded. I mean he can hardly see, he's got shrapnel inside him still, his wife's just died, and yet he's lovely and friendly. I have to help him find that cottage...I'm so worried about the effect it will have on him if we can't find it."

"We will. I'll come with you," said Juan. "I've been to Sicily a few times before; I might be able to help."

I smiled to myself at the thought of us: me - this extraordinarily overweight woman, Frank a 96-year-old widower and Juan Pedro, a flamboyant Spanish dancer - all trekking round looking for a house from the 1940s, while being watched all the way by a slightly angry-looking nurse in a brown dress.

"Yes, you should come," I said. "I'll talk to Frank - you should definitely come."

CHAPTER FIFTEEN: OFF TO SICILY

Finally, the day had come. I stood on deck as the boat docked in Sicily - looking out towards the clusters of houses nestled in the hill-tops in front of us. The thought of tracking down Frank's relatives made me tingle with anticipation. It would be so amazing if Marco and Alberto were still alive and Frank could meet them, shake hands and hand over the letters. I knew how much it would mean to him to make amends.

I looked up to see Janette pushing Frank towards me, he was sitting in his wheelchair looking incredibly dapper, dressed in a brown three piece suit that looked like it came from the 1930s along with very shiny shoes. In his lap he carried a hat and a cane. Like the suit, they looked like something out of a 1930s musical. We were just a burst of incidental music away from a chorus of singing in the rain.

"Wow, Frank," I said. "You look amazing."

"Well, I thought I better be prepared for anything. This is how Irene loved me to dress, so I thought it's how I should dress today."

"It's very hot out there though," I said. "Are you sure you won't be too warm like that?"

"I have tried telling him," said Janette, with her hands on her hips. "But he won't listen."

"I can handle a bit of heat," said Frank with a shake of his head, as if to indicate that his past involved more discomfort than a warm suit on a hot day could ever threaten.

"Howdy!" came a shout from the other side of the deck. I looked up to see Juan Pedro walking towards us, dressed like something out of gay pride march. He was wearing rainbow-coloured trousers in some sort of shiny material that gleamed as he walked, along with a flowery, Hawaiian style shirt in orange with red and white blossom on it. On his feet were these odd kind of winkle-pickers in a glittery material. He was carrying a man bag made of lime-green, crocodile material. Now I love people who are unconventional, I'm all in favour of people who don't look strictly normal, but I couldn't imagine what Frank would make of him, and I was slightly worried since this was very much Frank's day; a day on which we had to all behave in a way which wouldn't alarm or frighten him.

"Good lord alive," said Janette on seeing Juan Pedro close up.

"Frank, remember Juan Pedro?" I said.

"Very nice to see you again, son," said Frank, reaching out a trembling hand. Juan Pedro shook it and patted Frank on the back.

"Frank, I hope I can help today in locating your wife's cottage. If there's anything I can do, or – Janette – if you need any help pushing the wheelchair or anything, you just shout and I'm here for you."

"Thank you, that's very kind," said Frank, and I was reminded that Frank couldn't see well enough to judge Juan Pedro on his appearance. Just like he couldn't see how fat I was or how dull Janette looked. None of that mattered. He was just judging us on the way we behaved, and the way we treated him and each other. It gave me a shot of warmth, and reminded me that what matters is not how you look, but how you behave, how you treat people, and how kind you are. I felt a tear come into my eye, and instinctively gave both Juan Pedro and Janette a huge hug. Juan Pedro seemed delighted, Janette seemed alarmed, I was determined by the end of the day she would've softened a little bit and realised that we all just wanted to help.

Janette, being the only sensible person in the party by a considerable margin, was given the job of carrying the maps, and all the information that would help us track down where Irene had lived, and where we might start to find her family.

"In this part of the world people tend to stay living in the same house much more than we would in England," said Frank. "Houses are passed down through generations. It's really not uncommon for children to be living in the houses that their grandparents and even great grandparents bought."

"Great. Then let's hit the road."

"Absolutely," said Juan Pedro. "Follow me."

So the rather odd party of an enormous fat girl in loose-fitting separates, a man in rainbow-coloured trousers carrying a lime coloured clutch bag, an elderly man in a wheelchair dressed like he'd just dropped in from the 1930s, and a rather stout and unsmiling nurse in a starched brown dress, all headed off into Sicily for the day. It was, I admit, hard to see how this was going to work out well.

CHAPTER SIXTEEN: EVERYTHING'S CHANGED

We walked up to the main square and jumped into a cab. Well, I say 'jumped' - that's a bit of a lie...what with the wheelchair being folded up and Frank being manually lifted in, and me unable to get the seat belt round me, and none of us speaking a word of Italian...it was all rather a palaver if I'm honest, but we struggled on board, and off we set. Janette clutched the modern day map, and handed me the map from the 1940s to look after.

Frank entertained us all the way with his war-time stories.

"We were called the D-Day dodgers, you know," he said.

"The what?"

"Well D-Day took place while we were in Italy. Lady Astor said that we were in Italy to avoid D-Day. If she'd seen what we'd been through, she would have realised we'd all much have preferred to be at D-Day. We had a song that we sang to take the mickey out of it all, let me see whether I can remember it...it's to the tune of Lili Marlene. Here we go:

'We landed at Salerno,
holiday with pay,
Jerry got the band out
to help us on our way.
We all sang songs,
the beer was free.
We danced all the way through Italy.
We were the D-Day Dodgers, the men who dodged D-Day."

We all applauded heartily.

"Here is place," said the driver. "Corleone."

Frank looked through the window and his face fell. We were relying on a 90-odd-year-old man to remember the place from 70 years ago, and he clearly didn't recognise anything at all. The two maps looked vastly different from one another, so it wasn't hard to see why he was confused.

"Come on, let's get out and take a look around," I said, trying to fake confidence.

I looked over and caught Janette's eye. I knew exactly what she was thinking...we had no way of knowing how we were going to do this, but on the other hand we simply had to do it. We couldn't let Frank go back to England without finding the cottage, without saying his goodbyes and handing over the letters. He was an old man - he might never get this chance again.

We walked over to a small wall. "Let me have a look at that," said Janette, and I opened up the map from the 1940s, while she unfolded the current map. We laid them both out in front of us, across the wall.

On the 1940s map there was hardly anything - just a handful of houses and shops. Irene's cottage was circled. The modern day map featured a new road system, roundabouts, motorways and loads of houses, shops and offices that weren't there before.

"It looks to me," said Janette. "As if the cottage has gone. Look on this map - see that small hill there, well that must be here on the modern map." She pointed at the two maps and I saw what she meant.

"Yes," I said. "Look - there's the church spire. It looks like the cottage was there - I pointed to where the cottage should be...it was now a cafe next to a garage."

"Really?" said Juan. "You reckon it was turned into a cafe?"

While Juan came over to investigate the map, I went over to see Frank. He looked exhausted and sad, sitting there, barely able to see, listening to us talking about how the cottage - his only link to his wife's past - had disappeared.

"Come on, let's go and have a cup of tea," I said, seeing his face brighten up. "We'll go to that cafe over there while they are messing around with the maps and I'll get myself on Google to see what I can find."

"Good plan," said Frank. "I don't know about Google, but tea is an excellent idea."

We sat down at a rickety old table, and the others joined us. Juan had pulled out a pen and was jotting down numbers.

"Are you doing your tax return?" I asked.

"Map coordinates," he replied, tapping the side of his head. "Right, OK. Got it."

"Got what?"

"These are the map coordinates of the cottage we're looking for." He pointed to the map from the 1940s with the cottage clearly marked on it. "And this is where the coordinates fall on this map."

We all looked down. Juan was pointing to the cafe.

"The family must have sold the cottage to a developer who built this cafe," said Janette, scratching her head and looking at the map.

Frank looked up and around the cafe, as if hoping to see something that would remind him of the past.

I called the waiter over and asked him, in my best Italian, whether this used to be a cottage. It was no good, my broken Italian and his lack of English was getting us nowhere.

"Wait minute," he said, rushing into the back of the cafe and emerging with a very handsome young man.

"How can I help you?" he said in near perfect English.

Janette clapped her hands together in relief. She went through our questions again, laying the maps out on the table. The guy looked through them and confirmed that this did look to be the spot that we were looking for, but it was never a cottage.

"My parents owned this cafe when I was born, so it's been a cafe for a long time," he said. He shouted out in Italian to his mother who came out and stood next to him, looking at the maps and chatting to him in Italian. Then she called someone's name and a man came in from the kitchens in a white overall.

"My parents say that they bought this cafe 20 years ago. It was already a cafe when they bought it," said the young man.

"Damn," said Juan Pedro. "No cottage here?"

"No cottage," they confirmed.

"But it does look like the right area, doesn't it?" said Juan.

The young man nodded as he studied the two maps.

"Let me try another tack," said Juan, beckoning over the English-speaking man. "Do you have any documentation from when you bought the cafe? I wonder who sold this property to you. Maybe we can track them down?"

"I will take a look," he said.

The man disappeared for so long that we thought he wasn't coming back, but to our delight and surprise he re-emerged with a piece of paper; the purchase agreement from when they bought the cafe two decades ago.

"My mother keeps everything," he said.

The name of the person they had bought the cafe from was Monsieur Dalmeny.

"I've never heard of him," said Frank.

There was an address next to it.

"Do you have a phone number?" I asked.

"No phone number here," he said.

"OK, then, we'll go there," I announced, standing up. I was conscious that we didn't have much time if we were going to get back to the ship by 5pm.

"Your best bet is to head on the main road. Where is your car?"

"We don't have a car. We'll need to get a taxi," I said.

"No problem," said the man. "I will take you there."

"Really? That would be amazing. Thanks so much," I said, and the four of us climbed (Janette), waddled (me), sashayed (Juan Pedro) and were lifted (Frank) into the car and the man, who we discovered was called Andreas, dropped us at the end of a pathway which led to the house of Monsieur Dalmeny - the man who'd sold them the cafe.

"Thank you so much," I said. "You've been very generous. Can I give you some money?"

"No, not at all," he said. "I'm just helping. Here is my number...please call if I can do anything else."

So, there we were then, wandering down a path to knock on some stranger's door and ask them what they remembered about the time they sold a cafe.

The house was quite plush, much posher than the other houses in this heavily rundown part of the country. Two goats wandered outside and children's toys were scattered on the lawns. Despite the paraphernalia of family life dotted around the place, it had the feeling of a house that was totally empty.

I knocked. The four of us stood there in silence. I knocked again. Still nothing.

Damn.

It was hard to know what to do next. We were really starting to run out of time, but I was aware of just how much Frank wanted to track down anyone related to the family that he felt he had let down so many years ago.

"I'll put a note through the door and see whether they respond to it. I'll put my phone number on and they can call me when they get back."

"It's 3pm," whispered Juan Pedro. "We're really running out of time here."

I knew he was right. We needed to be back in the vicinity of the boat by 5 o'clock, in order to make sure we had enough time to sort Frank out and get onto the ship before it left at 6pm.

"We're going to have to go soon, aren't we?" I said. Juan Pedro nodded gently.

I turned to Janette: "What do you want to do?" I asked.

She agreed that we ought to start heading back to the ship, and that Frank would have to send the letters once they'd tracked the family down. Janette leaned over to talk to Frank. He wanted more than anything to pass the letters on personally and talk to the family himself, but he knew that there was no time today to do that. "Let's go," he said, his voice barely a whisper and I felt like we'd all really let him down. I just hadn't thought about how difficult it would be; how much everything would have changed, and how hard it would be to find anyone who even knew Irene's family, let alone knew where they were now.

To add to our woes, it turned out that getting a cab back was easier said than done. I rang the number for the taxi company and was told by a surly Italian that it would be half an hour before they could get one to us.

"Okay," I said. "But we're heading back to the dock to get a ship, so it can't be any longer than that. Will it definitely be here in half an hour?"

"Yes it will be," confirmed the cab lady. We sat down on the edge of the grass and talked about how we must all work together once we got back to Britain to try and locate this family. I looked at my watch. It had been 40 minutes and there was no sign of the cab. I rang the company again and the woman assured me that it was 10 minutes away.

"It's 10 to 4," said Juan Pedro.

"I know, but what can I do? Shall I try calling Andreas at the cafe and see whether he can take us back to the harbour?"

"Yes, do that. If we miss this ship I'll be shot," said Juan. "I'm supposed to be dancing in the razzmatazz ball tonight."

"We won't miss the ship. It will be tight, but will get there,"" I said with a ridiculous amount of confidence considering there was no sign of a taxi anywhere, and I was struggling to get through to Andreas. An answerphone came on and I left a message, explaining we were the guys who he'd given a lift to earlier, and we were stuck.

We waited another 30 minutes – no cab, no reply from Andreas. It was now almost half past four and the journey would take at least an hour. Unless the cab came within the next 15 minutes we were in serious danger of not making the boat.

Finally, finally, a cab came round the corner and we clambered on board. I tried to tell the driver how much of a rush we were in, but he didn't seem to understand.

"Don't worry," he kept saying as we drove at unbelievably slow speeds through the narrow roads, coming up against obstacle after obstacle...there was far more traffic than there had been on our way up which slowed us down considerably; there were animals in the road as they were being taken from one field to another, then, just as we thought we were there, a diversion which cost us 15 minutes.

We arrived near the docks at five to six. While Janette got the wheelchair out of the car and put Frank into it, Juan Pedro and I ran as fast as we could towards the ship, hoping to alert them to our presence, and encourage them to wait. But it was too late. By the time we actually reached the boat, out of breath and dishevelled, it was 6.15 and our floating hotel was pulling out of the harbour. On the deck, many of the crew and passengers were gathered. Captain Homarus and Claire were there, along with Simon, waving furiously and shouting my name.

"Mary, Mary," he cried. "Get on the boat."

"How in God's name am I supposed to do that?" I said. "Swim out to it?"

I glanced at Juan Pedro. "Shall I?" he said. "Maybe I should swim to it to save my career."

"No, you nutter," I said. "Look how far it is now. Come on - let's go and find Frank and Janette."

So the two of us walked back towards our 96-year-old friend while a man I once dated for a few weeks screamed at me. "You must get on the boat". "You've only just recovered from the leprosy. Make sure you don't get ill again. Get on the boat."

"Leprosy?" said Janette.

"Long story," I replied.

CHAPTER SEVENTEEN: AWOL FROM THE SHIP

Just to recap...there was an ancient man in an ancient suit, a nurse in a brown dress, a fat lady in sandals that were hurting her feet and a spruced up Spanish dancer - all standing on the quayside with no provisions and no luggage while the ship they were meant to be on sailed away.

"Well, this is turning into quite an adventure, isn't it?" said Frank with a smile.

There was no doubting that.

"The good news is that we have another day in Sicily to find the Corleone family," I said. "I suppose that has to be a really great thing when you think about it."

"Yes," said Janette. "Let's look on the bright side; that's very good news, isn't it, Frank?"

I glanced down at our elderly friend; he looked absolutely exhausted.

"Let's find a hotel as near as possible to where we were earlier," said Juan Pedro. "You Google the area, Mary, and see whether you can find a hotel anywhere, and I'll ring some of the guys on the ship and see what's the best thing for us to do now. The ship goes to Naples next. Maybe we should spend the morning tracking Irene's family, then head to Naples and get on the ship when it docks there?"

"Yes, good plan," I said, feeling a little more relaxed now that there was a plan of some kind, even if it was a plan that involved a trek across Italy with a wheelchair-bound nonagenarian.

Juan Pedro picked up his phone to call people on the ship while I found a couple of hotels near the cafe, and left messages on answerphones.

"We are okay," said Juan Pedro with a huge sigh. "They said it will be quite simple for us to get back to Naples tomorrow and jump on the ship there. It leaves at 6pm again though, so we must be there this time."

"Great," I said, just as my phone rang. "Oh good, this will be the hotel now."

"Hello, Mary speaking."

"Hello," came a rather gruff voice. "Is Dalmeny here. You put note about buying the cafe under my door. You said someone from the cafe have senting you?"

"Oh yes!" I said. "Thank you so much for calling back. We really want to come and talk to you about it."

"Okay, come now," he said. "I am in house."

"Great," I said. "We're on our way." I hung up, explaining to the group what we would do, and calling for a taxi once more. If we could sort this out tonight, it would make getting to Naples tomorrow a hell of a lot easier. Things were starting to look good. This time the taxi came very quickly and we clambered on board. Once we were in it my phone rang. It was Andreas from the cafe returning my call.

"Don't worry, everything's fine," I told him. "We don't need a lift anymore and things are looking really good. I'll let you know how it all goes."

We reached the house and I was awash with positive feelings. The goats still grazed outside, and Dalmeny stood in the doorway. He was a large, heavily-built, bearded man with hands the size of laptop computers and as hairy as a bear's. He invited us in and I explained what we were trying to do, and showed him the map – both the one from 1940 and the current one. He put on his glasses and looked carefully from one map to the next, and agreed that it looked as if the cafe was currently where the old cottage used to be.

Great, I thought. *He agrees with us, he's going to help us.*

"I can't help you," he said.

Brilliant.

"Why not?" asked Juan.

"I know not anything for cafe," he said.

"Is there anyone who might know?" I tried. "We're really keen to get someone to help us. I'm trying to track down the Corleone family – Alberto Corleone?"

"I don't know them. Maybe my mother know. Come back tomorrow," he said.

"What time will she be here?"

"Maybe come back middle of day," he said.

"Okay. We have to be in Naples by 5pm though," I said. "Is there any chance we can come earlier perhaps?"

"No she not earlier," he said.

"Is there any way we can call your mum?"

"Tomorrow," he said. "My English not good. My wife here tomorrow. Her English good. My mother will know, my wife will help," he said

"OK. And when will your wife be here?" I asked.

"Middle of day with mother."

It seemed fairly conclusive that we didn't have a chance of getting any more information out of them until midday, so we wended our weary way, out of the house, past the goats and onto the main road. Luckily he was able to point us in the direction of a local bed-and-breakfast. By the time we arrived, Frank was exhausted, so he and Janette went up to their rooms. Juan and I were also exhausted but decided that it would be much more sensible to sit up drinking beer all night instead of going to bed. So we sat outside in the warm evening air and drank beer, ate breadsticks and tried to make sense of the whole thing.

"We have to find this cottage, Juan," I said. "You saw Frank's face today - he looked destroyed. We have to find it. How has no one heard of this family? I thought it was a tight-knit community?"

"They might have moved out years ago, though. They could have moved 50 years ago for all we know."

"Yes, I guess," I said, looking at Juan. He didn't look quite himself. "Are you worried about what the captain will say when we get back to the boat tomorrow?"

"I will be shot," said Juan, dramatically. "You wait and see...they will shoot me like a dog because I miss the ship."

He grimaced as he wiped bread crumbs off his shiny, rainbow coloured trousers and shook his head with an artistic flourish. "I have to be there tomorrow. I am leading the cha-cha-cha in the evening. Who will do it if I'm not there? I can't see Captain Homarus doing it. Can you?"

"You won't miss the boat tomorrow...everything will be OK."

CHAPTER EIGHTEEN: THE LONG-AWAITED MEETING

The next morning I awoke, bursting with energy, and walked down to breakfast utterly determined that we would find Irene's relatives if it was the last thing we did. I arrived in the breakfast room first and was instantly dismayed by the food on offer. I'd been so spoilt on the ship with luxurious buffets every day that the sight of a plate of pastries and rather mouldy-looking cheese made me feel quite unwell.

Still, I had to keep my strength up, so I managed to force three croissants down me, along with coffee that was so strong it made me shoot up out of my seat. By the time the others arrived, I had discovered they had pain au chocolate round the other side, and was burrowing my way through those.

We headed off at 11.30am to go back over to the house. I'd called a cab and we assembled ready to climb in and begin our day's searching. "This is it," I said to Frank. "I'm confident we'll find Irene's relatives today."

Despite a long night's sleep, he still looked exhausted. I noticed he hadn't eaten anything at breakfast. I knew we could do with getting him back onto the ship as soon as possible.

We were back at the big house by 11.50pm, and were let into a much noisier home than the one we'd visited the day before. Children played on the lawn outside and a baby cried upstairs.

"My wife soon back," we were told, and we set ourselves down in the kitchen while our host went to see to the baby.

By 12.30pm, we were becoming a little worried.

"My wife is come 2pm," he said.

"Oh no," I said, trying not to catch Juan's eyes. I'd promised him we'd be back on the boat by 5pm, but that would be impossible the way things were going. In the end, we heard a key in the front door at 2:30pm and a small, slim woman with long, wavy brown hair walked in. She didn't look unlike the picture that Frank had shown us of Irene, and for one almighty moment, I thought that she might be related, and we might sew up this whole mystery once and for all. It turned out that she wasn't in any way related to Irene and it was just pure coincidence that she vaguely looked like her. "Clutching at straws, darling," was how Juan described it.

She was really helpful, though, and had all the paperwork which showed that she bought the cottage from Alberto.

"Irene's brother," said Janette, breathlessly, leaning down to explain to Frank.

"I remember that he was selling it because his parents had died and he was living in his wife's parents' old house, or something like that," she said.

"Have you got any details about where the man you bought it from was living?" I asked. Holding my breath for the answer.

"Yes – it's here," she said. I'll write it down for you. In beautiful italic script, she wrote down an address. It was about half an hour away.

"If we go there, we will miss the flight," I said, and I heard Juan emit a small shriek, like the sort of noise you hear when air is escaping from a tightly pulled balloon. I decided to ignore it and look at Janette.

"Let's stay in Sicily for another night then go straight to La Spezia tomorrow, missing out Naples completely," I said.

"OK," said Janette. "If that's OK with you two?"

"Oh fine, no problem at all with me," said Juan. "Don't worry about the cha-cha-cha or the ballet spectacular."

I elbowed him in the ribs to silence him.

"Let's book back into the bed and breakfast," said Janette.

"Sure," I responded. "We'll go back there so Frank can have a lie down, and I'll ring the phone number on the sheet and we'll head off to see them later this afternoon."

It seemed that finally, finally, we were getting closer to Irene's family.

We said our goodbyes and thanked them very much for their help. When I looked down at Frank, he looked nervous.

"Everything OK?" I asked.

"Everything's fine dear," he said. "I'll be glad when this is all done though. It's been a long time since I saw her family. A very long time."

As we headed out into the bright sunshine, I realised what a difficult thing this must be. I'd appreciated how important it was, but didn't realise how difficult. Frank was about to confront issues that had lain dormant for decades. I smiled at him and called the number on the sheet, bracing myself for the sound of Alberto's voice...Irene's brother...the man they'd had to flee Italy to avoid. Rather anti-climaxically, it went straight to answerphone. I couldn't leave a message...I had no idea how to begin describing what was happening. "I'll just keep trying," I explained to Frank. "Don't worry – we'll get hold of them and we'll go and see them. Juan – do you want to ring the guys on the boat and explain that we'll be there tomorrow evening instead?"

"Sure," he said, with a shrug. "That'll be a nice easy call to make."

Juan walked off, pouting and sulking, and the rest of us waited on the edge of the road for a taxi. I wish I'd known about all this before I left England. It would have been so much easier to get on the main computer at home and start searching than it was to sit on roadsides in Sicily trying to get a signal in the blasting midday sun while waiting for taxis.

It would also, with hindsight, have been much easier to have hired a car.

In the end, it was the next day before I got an answer on the phone. I'd paced around all evening, reassuring Juan that he wouldn't lose his job, and reassuring Janette that we would find the relatives and Frank would be able to hand over the letters. I'd been updating the blog with all the ins and outs of our battle to find the cottage, and Dawn – who never issues an iota of praise to anyone, came back to say how much she loved the updates. It was a bright moment in quite a tense few days.

When I finally got an answer on the phone the next morning, I was relieved that it was a young-sounding man who spoke English. I explained, as best I could, who we were and what we wanted and he replied that he had heard of Irene and he knew the story of her running away with Frank. He said his name was Louis and he was Alberto's grandson. I smiled from ear-to-ear. We'd found them.

"I will get my mother," he said.

A lady called Gisella came to the phone and said that she was Alberto's daughter.

"Irene was my aunt," she said. "She wrote to us all the time, we heard from her on birthdays and at Christmas, but we never saw her. I never, ever met her. While my grandparents were alive, she visited them but that was it. It would be lovely to meet Frank...she wrote about him so lovingly in her letters."

"One final question," I said. "Is Alberto still alive?"

"Yes," she said. "He is in a nursing home. I will take you to see him."

"Oh my Goodness," said Frank when I told him. "Oh my goodness. We've done it. We've found him. I'll get to talk to Alberto, after all these years."

Visiting time at the nursing home was in the mornings. I tried explaining that we'd come so far to see him, but it was no good. We would have to stay another night in Sicily, miss out the Toulon stage of the trip and rejoin the cruise in Barcelona. It was the only way. I looked over at Juan.

"That's the Viennese Waltz gone then," he said. "And someone else will have to judge the grannies tap dance competition. And I'll need to buy clothes. It's getting ridiculous."

"Yes, we can go shopping this afternoon, buy some new clothes, then go and visit Alberto tomorrow morning before heading for Barcelona. You'll need to let them know on the ship though."

Juan looked ashen at the thought. "They'll tie me up and beat me til I'm dead," he said. "Or they'll roast me alive and put me on the buffet table."

"No they won't," I said. "They'll be mildly pissed off, then they'll get over it."

Juan made the call.

"No," he assured, them, for the third day in succession. "We will not miss the boat in Barcelona, definitely. I promise you." Then he put the phone down and smiled at me. "He said your blog's very good. They are keeping up with our progress through that. I must take a look at it when we get back on board"

"Oh good," I said, remembering that I'd described Juan's clothing in great detail and diarised all his pouting, huffs and stomps off to the corner when he didn't get his own way. To be fair though, I had also said how kind, warm and generous he was, and what a credit to the cruise company. Hopefully he'd focus on those comments, and not dwell on my descriptions of his vile trousers and ridiculous green handbag.

The next morning we all assembled for breakfast dressed in 'I am love Sicily' t-shirts. It had turned out there were no clothes shops anywhere near, so we were forced to buy the only t-shirts that the gift shop had. Mine was turquoise, Frank's was white, Janette's was navy and Juan's was yellow. We looked like Sicily's entry for the Eurovision Song contest when we walked next to one another.

"It would be bad enough if they said 'I love Sicily'," said Janette. "But to say 'I am love Sicily' is just ridiculous."

"Oh God," cried Juan. "I hadn't noticed that."

We headed for the house that Frank's daughter and grandchildren lived in, and Gisella took us straight to the nursing home. She explained that she and her children had moved into her mum and dad's house with them. "We needed to look after dad," she explained. "He fell apart a bit when mum died."

"I know that feeling," said Frank, and Janette touched his shoulder gently.

The nursing home was cramped and stuffy, and like every other building housing lots of people, it smelled faintly of cabbage.

"Reminds me of school dinners," said Janette, as we walked along the corridor towards Alberto's room.

"I couldn't call him to tell him we were coming because he's not really up to using the phone," said Gisella. "I'll go in first and explain."

"Of course," said Frank. "Don't want to terrify him."

We watched as she knocked gently, and then went into his room, talking in Italian. None of us could speak the language but we heard her say 'Frank' and 'Irene' in the midst of the unfamiliar, foreign words.

"He says to come in," said Gisella.

I glanced at Janette and she smiled, as she pushed the wheelchair through the door. I wasn't sure whether to follow or stay where I was, so I opted for following.

"Shall I come in?" asked Juan.

"Yes," I said. "Let's support Frank."

Inside the room was a desperately thin old man. He was scrawny and pale as he lay back on the sheets.

"You haven't changed a bit," said Frank.

"You neither," said Alberto in a strong Italian accent but very clear English. "Just the same."

Then the two men laughed. Last time they'd seen one another they had been soldiers; strong, young men in their prime.

"I've waited all these years to apologise to you," said Frank. "What I did...it was terrible. Taking your sister away with no explanation."

"It wasn't terrible," said Alberto. "We all understood. You made Irene so happy. How could I be angry?"

"How do you know I made her happy? We all lost contact."

"My mother showed me all the letters that Irene sent. We knew she was well looked after...we knew she was happy with you, so we were happy too."

"Irene wrote to you, too, but never sent the letters. She was so worried that you would come over to England and find us, in those early years, when we were settling down to our new life together, so she just kept them all. I found them after she died. I'd like you to have them."

Janette opened the bag and handed piles of letters to Gisella.

"I'll read them to you," Gisella told her father.

"Yes please," said Alberto, his voice very weak. "How lovely of you to bring them after all these years."

"What happened to Marco?" asked Frank.

"He ran off with another local girl as soon as Irene had gone. He got her pregnant and left the area, leaving her to bring up the child alone. No one heard from Marco again. Irene made the right choice in you, Frank. Marco was no good; I think we all knew that deep down. Thank you for looking after her."

Frank wheeled his chair close to the bed and reached out to take Alberto's hand.

"Thank you," he said. "Thank you for your strength and thank you for not being bitter. Irene was my life. We were very happy, Thank you for understanding."

Alberto smiled and closed his eyes.

"He's tired now," said Gisella. "We should go."

We all walked out of the room except for Frank who stayed a moment longer, before following us.

"Thank you all. Thank you so much," he said, with tears streaming down his face. "I wish I'd come here years ago, with Irene. I feel like a weight has lifted off me."

CHAPTER NINETEEN: FACING SIMON

"We are in Spain. Viva L'Espania," said Juan Pedro, mincing off the plane like he was walking on stage. "Everyone - follow me."

Janette raised her eyebrows and signalled for me to go after him. She would wait until the airline staff brought the wheelchair to them so that Frank could be taken off.

"See you out there," I said.

I caught up with Juan Pedro to see him pouting into the frosted glass windows. "My lips have shrunk," he said.

"No, they haven't," I replied. "Maybe your brain has shrunk, but certainly not your lips."

"Oy!" he said, interlacing his arm through mine, like we were two teenagers in an American soap. "I think we should go clothes shopping. Spanish clothes are the best."

"Yeah, no native dress though. I'm not looking like an idiot again."

"OK, we just go to fashionable modern shops then."

"I'm not going to Zara though," I said. I knew Zara was Spanish and I also knew that their clothes were evil. Even their XL was about three sizes too small for me - it was the most depressing shop on earth.

"No Zara," he reassured. "We will go to a fabulous designer market. You will love it. It's full of gays."

"Oh great," I said. "I'm glad you think I'd love that. What do you think I am - some sort of fag hag?"

"Why yes - but not any sort of fag hag. You are MY fag hag."

"We need to wait for Frank, though. I don't think he'll want to go clothes shopping in a gay designer market after everything he's been through, but I want to make sure he's OK."

We waited for them to appear. "Frank's exhausted, so we're going to head straight back to the ship," said Janette. "We'll catch up with you two later."

"We won't be long; I'm exhausted too," I said.

"Whatever you do - don't miss the ship again," said Janette, and the two of them headed off.

"I think Frank might be one of the nicest people I've ever met," I said to Juan and he smiled in reply. "A very,

very cool man," he agreed, then off we went to go shopping.

I followed Juan around like a little puppy, weaving in and out of the racks behind him, while he picked out clothes he thought would be suitable for me. "Right—boyfriend jeans—you need these," he said. "We also want some skinny jeans, and I think some cropped white jeans would look good." He called over the assistant, who he knew by name. The two of them talked together, looking over at me, before the lady went off and came back with armfuls of clothes.

"Right, follow me," said Juan, leading me towards the changing rooms with his haul of clothing. "In you go...tell me what you think."

I slipped the boyfriend jeans on first; they were just lovely, quite loose-fitting and really comfortable, as well as looking good. "You really know your stuff, don't you?" I said.

"This is coming as a surprise to you?" he replied sarcastically.

"Try the white jeans on. I know you won't really like them, because they are tight-fitting, but they are more stylish than those awful ones you had on the other day. These ooze style and you can wear them with either flats or high heels."

With everything I tried on, I emerged from the changing room to comments, prodding and, on a couple of occasions, a round of applause from Juan. We were making quite a commotion in our matching Sicily shirts, but it didn't seem to matter. Juan had this effect on everyone; everywhere he went he was the centre of attention without ever seeming to try.

"Will you try those skinny jeans on with this white shirt?" asked Juan, handing a soft white shirt to me.

I put the white shirt on and tucked it into the jeans, slipping on a pair of high-heel boots that Juan had suggested. I looked in the mirror and, even though I felt uncomfortable in tight jeans, given the size of my massive bottom, I looked good; much better than I usually do. I walked out of the changing room, spinning around in front of Juan.

"You look very beautiful," said an English voice. I looked up, and right in front of me, staring straight at me, was Simon.

"Hello," I said, flustered. "Let me introduce Juan."

Juan put out his hand and gently shook Simon's.

"I'm going to get jumpers," he said, running off to the other side of the store.

"Sorry we haven't had the chance to talk properly," I said. "I wanted to come and explain...I recovered from the illness. I'm much better now."

"I can see that," said Simon. "I'm so relieved. I always wondered what happened. It's good to see you looking so well."

"Thank you, you too," I said. "We should catch up for a drink later, when we're all back on board."

"Sure, I'd like that," he said. "I've been reading your blog. Frank sounds amazing. Will you introduce me to him later?"

"Of course," I said, looking out across the rails and seeing Juan, ducked down, hiding behind the bikinis.

"Well, see you later then," said Simon, and he wandered off.

"Come back here now," I shouted over to Juan.

"Sorry - but you needed to talk...you can't just ignore him all the time."

"No, I know - well we've talked now. I told him I recovered from leprosy and he was very pleased."

"Nutter," said Juan. "Absolute nutter."

By the time we returned to the ship I had seen nothing of Barcelona bar the biggest indoor market ever - it was astonishing. I had bags full of clothes, plus a pair of earrings that Bet Lynch would have thought too garish and a pair of pink boots that I knew I will never wear, but with Juan there, egging me on, it had seemed such a good idea.

Juan was in his element...trying loads of things on – coming out of the changing rooms, spinning round and pouting like a model. He had about three bags of clothing, all sold to him at bargain prices because of his astonishing ability to haggle.

We boarded the boat, much to the captain's delight, and I headed straight for my cabin – collapsing onto the bed with exhaustion. It had been the most draining experience – physically and emotionally. I could only imagine how Frank must be feeling.

I'd kept the blog up-to-date throughout the trip...I just needed to add on a final update to the story then I could have a quick sleep before supper.

I sent several texts to Dawn, then had a shower and lay back on the bed. I'd taken a few pictures while out and about in Sicily, but fewer than I had on other days because it was such an intensely personal crusade for Frank, I didn't want to be intrusive; Frank didn't deserve that.

I decided to go onto the blog to see how it all looked on there, and whether there was any reaction from anyone.

I called up the site and waited for it to load. My God! There were loads of responses. Thousands of people had been following Frank's story. The whole thing was astonishing. Even an MP had commented.

"Our war heroes are very special people indeed. They should be honoured."

There were hundreds of messages underneath the MP's.

"Help them get home!" said one.

"Send the army out to help him find the cottage!" said another.

"Knight him!"

It had never occurred to me before that the blog might have been a good way of summoning help. When we were wandering, helplessly, through the Sicilian countryside, it would have been useful to know that thousands of people were following us, willing us on.

I felt too wide-awake to sleep, so I decided to get ready for dinner nice and slowly, really taking my time. I slipped on the huge earrings, looked in the mirror, realised I looked completely ridiculous, and took them off again. Then, finally happy that I didn't look insane, I went out for to join the others in the bar. I'd been told that we all had to gather for 7pm that evening, and when we met I would understand why.

I wandered into the bar area and as I walked in everyone cheered and clapped. Juan walked in next and they cheered him as well, and when Frank and Janette came in there was the loudest cheer I'd ever heard. It was like being at a football stadium or something. People were clapping, banging the tables and cheering like mad.

"Frank, Frank, Frank," they chorused.

Frank and Janette stood in the middle of it all, looking utterly confused.

"What's going on?" Frank asked.

"They are cheering us for our expedition, and cheering Frank because he's so incredible," I said.

"How did they know about our expedition? Did you tell them?" asked Janette.

"No, I assumed you had," I said.

"No," said Janette. "It must have been Juan." We both looked at him.

"Not me," he said.

"Ladies and gentlemen, can I have your attention?" said Captain Homarus. "You've all given the most tremendous welcome to Frank, Juan, Janette and Mary, and I'd like to say just a couple of words. You've managed to miss the ship three times; you've caused mayhem and great worry and panic here..."

Everyone laughed as he spoke.

"But we have been following the blog and we are overwhelmed by Frank's story. We've learned all about your incredible war service, and how you lost your friends at Longstop Hill, we've heard about your life as a D-Day Dodger and evading capture once, only to be captured again and be forced to spend two years in a horrific Prisoner of War camp. And we've heard about Irene...the amazing woman who you loved so much. Irene must have loved you a great deal too, Frank, to have left her family like that. I think we all understand why you wanted to go back and find her family and we're so glad you found them and that all is well. You are an amazing man and we'd all like to raise our glasses to you."

There were tears in Frank's eyes and his hand shook as Claire handed him a glass of champagne. He raised the glass slowly and sipped it, putting his hand out to shake Captain Homarus's hand, and waving his thanks to the assembled throng.

"Tell me - what is this 'blog'?" he asked.

"Well, Frank, a blog is a story that someone called Dawn has written all about you - to tell the world about your incredible life and the incredible journey you have just been on."

"Who is Dawn?" asked Frank.

"I think we all know that Mary is Dawn," said the captain.

"No - Dawn's in the cabin," I started saying.

"No, you're the one who's been writing this wonderful blog, and you're the one who deserves all the praise."

"So, I didn't manage to convince you that Dawn was in the cabin, then?"

"No, of course not. We knew she wasn't on the ship because she never checked in."

"Oh."

"The blog's great. You're really talented," said the captain. "Shall I escort you into dinner?"

"Gosh, thank you," I replied.

CHAPTER TWENTY: VALENCIA WITH JUAN

Another day, another amazing city...the last stop on the cruise. It was incredible to think it was all coming to an end. It had been more astonishing than I could ever have imagined.

We pulled into the port of Valencia and Juan Pedro raised his arms triumphantly. This was his home city, where he had grown up and learned to dance before his burgeoning profession took him to Paris, then to New York, then to the open seas as head dancer on the cruise ship.

He had promised to take me around his city and tell me all about it...unveil all the hidden treasures that normal tourists never see... but when I met him on the deck he seemed unusually pensive and not as exuberant as I was expecting.

"Everything OK?" I asked.

"Well, yes," he said, but it really didn't sound as if everything was OK.

"You sure?"

"Yes, everything is fine, but when I come to Valencia I always think of Javier. He was my one true love. He was a great dancer. We performed together for Ballet Valencia and I haven't seen him in years. Last time we met we made out up against the wall outside the men's toilets. It was wonderful"

"Yeah, it doesn't have quite the romance of Frank's story, does it?"

"It was romantic in its own way," he says, with an extravagant toss of his head. "May be I will pop in to Ballet Valencia and if he is there, I will say hello, if not – then it was not meant to be."

"Sounds like a good plan. What shall we do first?"

"In Valencia? Why – first we eat."

It turned out that Valencia was the perfect place to have a day to wander around. We spent an hour or so exploring the old town, before a lunch in Casa Montana - one of the oldest restaurants in Valencia. We ate in the busy front bar, lined with wine barrels, and enjoyed big fried anchovies, brown broad beans stewed with chorizo, roasted piquillo peppers stuffed with béchamel and tuna, and jamón ibérico. I wanted fries as well, but Juan said that was tacky. Coming from a man in tight leather trousers that finished half way up his calf, I wasn't sure whether that was a compliment or an insult.

After lunch we went to the cathedral which was just mind blowing. We saw San Vincente's withered left arm and two Goya paintings, one of which showed a horrifying exorcism and which Juan seemed particularly fond of. He remembered going there as a schoolboy and being mesmerized by it. The guide came along and told us that the windows were made from fine alabaster, because Valencia's light is too dazzling for glass. I know this all sounds quite dull, and a bit 'touristy', but I enjoyed every minute.

We went into Ballet Valencia but there was no sign of Juan's lover – apparently he had gone on tour with the company to New York. "I will see him there," said Juan.

"Yes, I've heard the walls next to the men's toilets are nice there," I said.

We then wandered down to the beach for a little siesta – lying back on the sand and looking up at the blue skies.

"I don't want to go home," I said.

"Then don't," he replied. "Get a job on a cruise ship and tour the world with me. We'll have the best time ever."

"No – I need to go back. My boyfriend, my mum, my dad, my job..."

"You hate your job," he said.

"Well that's true, but I have to do it or I won't be able to afford to eat...and I do like to eat."

"Ha, you're a nutter. Come and live on a cruise ship and you'll have all the food you could ever want."

As Juan spoke, I heard my phone ring in my bag.

"Hi, Mary speaking," I said.

"Mary, it's Janette here. Are you on the boat anywhere?"

"No, I'm lying on the beach with a ridiculously skinny gay man called Juan. Why? Everything OK?"

"Not really," she said. "Frank's been taken ill."

CHAPTER TWENTY-ONE: CONCERNED ABOUT FRANK

Juan and I leaped to our feet, grabbed our bags and raced like lunatics through the streets of Valencia, back towards the harbour and onto the ship. The boat was eerily quiet while it was in port. Everyone was making the most of the sunshine and the markets in Valencia. Everyone, that is, except for Frank.

I ran onto the deck and bumped into Claire. "Where is Frank?" I asked.

"Come with me," she said, leading me through to the medical rooms.

"Just wait here minute." She disappeared behind a closed door, and I heard voices, then Janette came out.

"What is the matter?" I said. "Is he okay?"

"He is fine, I think he's just exhausted," said Janette. "I was very worried about him when I called you because he seemed extraordinarily weak. I sometimes forget how old he is, our trip really took it out of him."

"Oh goodness, I feel terrible," I said. "We shouldn't have traipsed around like that; I just wanted him to be able to put his mind at rest, and hand over the letters."

"Absolutely," said Janette. "Please don't feel bad, what we did was amazing. I know we've made him a very, very happy man. He's just tired now, and needs to rest."

As we stood chatting, Captain Homarus walked into the room, and looked at me.

"Have you come to see a doctor?" he asked.

"No, just checking up on Frank."

"The doctor says he needs to rest, I suggest you give him a few hours, and maybe come down later if you want to see him, at that stage the doctors will know what is going on."

Janette and I walked out of the small surgery, back to the medical clinic, and out onto the main deck where Juan was sitting, waiting for us. "Why didn't you come in?" I said.

"I hate doctors," he grimaced. "They make me feel ill. Just can't stand them... The smell, the noise, the white coats..."

"There were no white coats, just Captain Homarus who told us to come back in a couple of hours."

"OK," said Juan. "When you go back, make sure you say hello from me. I promise you - I can't go down there, doctors give me the heebie-jeebies."

"OK, OK," I said. "No need to go down there then."

I turned to Janette: "Do you fancy getting off the boat for a bit?" I was aware that all she'd been doing was looking after Frank; she might fancy an hour in Valencia before going down to see him again.

"I'd love to go out and buy some new clothes. I thought you looked amazing after Juan took you shopping," she said.

"Whaaaat? Really? Are you taking the mickey?"

"No - really - those bright colours and that incredible jewellery. I'd love to dress like that, but I don't have the confidence."

"Then I shall take you shopping straight away. You see this, Mary - this is a woman who knows good taste when she sees it."

"That would be great," said Janette. "I can't leave the ship though...I have to be here incase anything happens to Frank."

"I'll be here," I said, suddenly. "I'll stay on board and if anything happens at all - I'll phone you straight away."

"Are you sure?" asked Janette.

"Of course I'm sure," I said. "Perfectly sure...off you go."

Once they had disappeared, I went back into the medical centre and made sure the doctor had my number incase anything happened, then I strode out onto the deck, to sit in the sunshine for a few hours and enjoy a gin and tonic.

CHAPTER TWENTY-TWO: HOME SWEET HOME

I popped back down to the medical centre later in the afternoon, but there was no news; Frank was stable and sleeping soundly. He wasn't in any grave danger, but he was weak, and the doctor planned to get him straight to Southampton Hospital when we arrived back.

I went back up to my cabin, texted Janette to update her and did some updates to the blog, then I dressed in a simple black evening dress and went and sat in the bar before dinner, hoping to see Juan and Janette.

Now, when I say 'hoping to see' - it was impossible not to see Janette. She walked into the room with all the style and glamour of Elizabeth Taylor in Cleopatra...and almost as much eyeliner. She'd been transformed. I mean - sure - she was completely over the top because this was Juan who was styling her, but she looked magnificent. I felt dowdy by comparison, and vowed to sneak back to the cabin and put more makeup on before dinner.

"You look sensational," I told her, hugging her.

"Thank you," she said, she really was beaming. "I love this outfit...I'm really chuffed. Isn't Juan amazing?"

"Don't talk about him like that," I said. "He'll get an even bigger head - we need to be bringing him down, not talking him up."

Dinner was called and the three of us sat together, hoping to sit alone and chat about Frank and everything we'd been through, but it was impossible. The entire ship was aware of Frank's illness. Concern and kindness had driven them to join us to enquire about him.

Arriving back in Southampton was a bitter-sweet moment. I was looking forward to seeing Ted again, and I was looking forward to seeing my friends and telling them all about my adventure, but I would miss these guys. It was strange to think how close we'd all become. I knew we'd be friends forever.

Frank was taken off the ship and put into an ambulance, moaning all the way that he was absolutely fine, and this was just a fuss about nothing, and how he fought in the war.

"Bye lovely," I said, hugging Janette and giving Juan a huge squeeze. "Let's stay in touch - OK?"

"Definitely," they agreed, and I strode back through the car park to where I could see Ted: lovely, kind Ted, waiting patiently.

"Hello there stranger," I said, giving him a big kiss, and loving the way he lifted me up into the air. "How are you?"

"I'm much happier now you're back," he said. "Come on; let's go home...I want to hear all about it. By the way - do you know that t-shirt makes no grammatical sense at all?"

"Yes, I know," I said. "But I love it – it reminds me of the most amazing time ever. Come on, I'll tell you all about it."

It was three days later when the call came through. I was back at work, stacking bags of compost in the outdoor plant section when my phone rang.

"Frank has died," said Janette, her voice croaky with pain and choked back tears. "He'd passed away peacefully in his sleep."

It was horrible news but at least Frank had died knowing that he'd made peace with the world, and now he was reunited with Irene. I hope he died knowing how much he affected my life and how much it meant to me to be with him on his Sicilian adventure.

I went to the funeral, of course, and met his friends who had all heard about our exploits in Sicily. Back at Frank's house, after the funeral, we raised our glasses and toasted the lovely man with a rendition of the song he'd sung to us on that crazy afternoon in Sicily:

'We landed at Salerno,
holiday with pay,
Jerry got the band out
to help us on our way.
We all sang songs,
the beer was free.
We danced all the way through Italy.
We were the D-Day Dodgers, the men who dodged D-Day."

Rest In Peace, Frank. They don't make 'em like you anymore...

Other books in the Adorable Fat Girl series:

Diary of an Adorable Fat Girl
Adventures of an Adorable Fat Girl
Crazy Life of an Adorable Fat Girl
Christmas with an Adorable Fat Girl
Adorable Fat Girl and her Weight loss Tips
Adorable Fat Girl on Safari
Cruise with an Adorable Fat Girl
Adorable Fat Girl takes up Yoga

Coming soon...

Adorable Fat Girl goes to Weightloss Camp
Adorable Fat Girl and the Mysterious Invitation

See: www.bernicebloom.com for details of all the 'Adorable Fat Girl' books.

Printed in Great Britain
by Amazon

65713430R00099